MAYBE MARRIED

BY

LEIGH MICHAELS

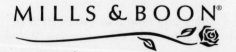

MILLS & BOON®

First published in Great Britain 2002
Large Print edition 2003
Harlequin Mills & Boon Limited,
Eton House, 18-24 Paradise Road,
Richmond, Surrey TW9 1SR

© Leigh Michaels 2002

ISBN 0 263 17887 0

Set in Times Roman 16½ on 17½ pt.
16-0303-50028

Printed and bound in Great Britain
by Antony Rowe Ltd, Chippenham, Wiltshire

MAYBE
MARRIED

CHAPTER ONE

A BURST of applause, followed by a low buzz of conversation and the telltale rustling of two dozen people rising from their chairs, told Dana that the meeting was over. Just in time, too, she thought. As long as no one hung around for prolonged goodbyes, they might still manage to keep to the schedule.

Beside her, Connie glanced at her watch. "It's past five. President Howell is cutting it a little fine, I'd say. But then he's not the one who has to clean up the damage—and he does like to hear himself talk."

Dana ignored both the comment and the sidelong look which accompanied it. "I'll start picking up the debris now. As soon as the last guest clears the doorway, you can start to vacuum at this end of the room. Tell the caterers they can begin setting up the bar in fifteen minutes." She didn't wait for an answer before she slid open the pocket door which separated the hallway from the drawing room and went in.

Originally, there had been two parlors oc-
cupying the entire width of the big Georgian
house. But years ago when the university had
bought the mansion as a home for its presi-
dents, the dividing wall had been knocked out
to make a single enormous room suitable for
entertaining crowds. In matching fireplaces at
each end of the room, gas logs flickered cheerfully, banishing the gloom of a dreary, rainy
late afternoon. Between the two sets of French
doors overlooking the veranda was a table
holding the ravaged remains of afternoon tea.
Dana noted almost automatically that the few
leftover cucumber sandwiches looked limp, the
strawberries had faded and shrunk, and the pe-
tits fours appeared hard as rocks. But then, it
was nearly three hours since the tea table had
been arranged.

At the far end of the room, nearest the front
door, a dozen women were still clustered
around the university's president. Dana heard
Barclay Howell's deep voice, though she
didn't catch what he'd said, followed by a
burst of feminine laughter.

Dana stayed as far away as she could, trying
to be unobtrusive as she gathered up stale coffee cups, dropped napkins, and—what was half

a scone doing under the edge of the love seat, anyway? Getting this room cleared out and ready for the cocktail party which was due to start in less than an hour was going to be an especially big challenge.

She didn't see Mrs. Janowitz until the matron was within five feet. "Dana, my dear," the woman said, bearing down on her. "Such a lovely party. I was just telling Barclay how much nicer the events here at Baron's Hill have been ever since you took over."

"Thank you, Mrs. Janowitz." Dana's hands were full, but the matron was between her and the doorway where Connie had parked the service cart, so she took a firmer grip on both the china and her patience.

"That so-called butler they had before," Mrs. Janowitz went on, "had no flair. No sense of style. He paid far too much attention to petty things and never looked at the big picture."

Dana felt obligated to give the woman a warning. "Mr. Beeler will be returning as soon as he's completely recovered from his pneumonia."

"Oh, yes, I know." Mrs. Janowitz's voice was airy. "You'd hardly want to keep on doing everything yourself. And I'm sure, with his fondness for detail, he'll be much better at carrying out instructions than in planning things all the way through."

"I'm not sure you understand. As soon as Mr. Beeler returns, I'll be going back to my regular job as manager of the conference center."

"If you want to call it a conference center, when it's really just an old classroom building." Mrs. Janowitz smiled broadly and patted Dana's arm. "But of course, my dear, I completely understand that's the official line for the moment. However, for those of us who can see what's really going on..." Her voice dropped. "We *approve,* Dana. I thought you'd like to know." She strode back across the room and plunged into the still-chattering group around Barclay Howell.

Dana shook her head and dumped the plates and cups she'd gathered onto the service cart. She had no idea what Mrs. Janowitz was talking about and no time to ponder the question at the moment. If President Howell didn't move these women out in a hurry, they were going to collide at the front door with his cocktail party guests.

As if he'd heard her, the president shepherded the remaining half dozen women into the hallway. Dana watched from the corner of her eye. She'd seen him do it countless times, but it still amazed her how easily Barclay Howell could maneuver people out the door without ever letting them realize they'd been politely sent on their way. Or at least he made it look easy. He'd no doubt had plenty of practice in the time he'd spent as a college administrator, working his way up the ladder to the president's office.

Connie appeared with the vacuum cleaner, which had been specially chosen for its low noise level rather than its cleaning power, and started on the carpet. Dana was just starting to push the service cart into the hall where it would be out of Connie's way when Barclay Howell came back into the room, dusting his hands together in satisfaction.

"Dana," he called. "I'd like a moment with you, privately."

Dana looked around the room. She still had to freshen up the flower arrangements and move them off the tea table so it could be torn down, and Connie could use help in shifting all the chairs. There was no time to spare for chitchat, but after all, Barclay Howell was the boss. "Let me get rid of this cart first."

"I'll be in the music room."

She pushed the cart down the hall toward the kitchen and then returned to the front of the house. Next to the front door, across the wide entrance hall from the drawing room, was a much smaller, more intimate room. She tapped on the half-open door and went in.

Barclay Howell was selecting music from a cabinet full of compact disks. He put one in the slot and the first notes of a violin concerto murmured through the room. "You did a wonderful job today, Dana," he said. "Every one of those women was thrilled with the meeting arrangements."

"Thank you." Dana frowned. "But I wonder why they were so pleased. There wasn't anything particularly original about anything I did today."

Barclay smiled broadly. "Dana, Dana. You must stop disparaging yourself."

"But in this case it's true, sir. Those women must have been to hundreds of afternoon teas, and this one wasn't any different, really. I wonder why they made it a point to tell you that." *We approve,* Mrs. Janowitz had said.

Dana was beginning to get a ticklish feeling in her stomach as she wondered just exactly what Mrs. Janowitz had meant. "Unless they were just being extra polite."

"No, it was more than that. You have a certain flair for these things. Sit down, Dana, and let's talk." He gestured toward a deeply-upholstered chair.

Dana was torn between wanting to stay and needing to go back to work. Pursuing this conversation right now was really going to ruin her schedule. On the other hand, this was the first chance she'd had to talk to Barclay Howell about anything more important than canapes.

Until the last six weeks, the university's president had been little more than a name to Dana. But since she'd started working directly with him at Baron's Hill, she'd begun to realize that he was a very attractive man—and not only because of his looks. Not that she knew him well enough to really judge, yet. But now, suddenly, he seemed to be starting to notice her on a personal level... The ticklish feeling grew stronger.

"The cocktail party," she began. "I really need to—"

"I'm sure your assistant can manage the details for a few minutes. If there's one small flaw in the way you handle things, Dana, it's that you insist on doing so much yourself rather than delegating it."

The professional half of her would have liked to point out that managing the details was what she'd been hired to do, that Connie was pitching in only because Dana needed help and not because it was Connie's job, and that Barclay Howell was making everything more difficult at the moment.

There were no doubt more tactful ways to make that point, but unfortunately just now Dana couldn't think of a single one. So she stayed silent.

"Ever since Beeler got sick and you took over, things here at Baron's Hill have been going much more smoothly. We've done almost twice as many events in the last six weeks as we usually do, but under your direction there hasn't been a single problem."

I wouldn't exactly say that, Dana thought. *The problems were there—you just didn't hear about them.*

"The entertainment has been superb, the food delicious, the guests happy."

And I'm exhausted.

"How would you like to have the job permanently?"

As he talked, Dana's stomach had slowly settled back into place. So much for the vague feeling that Barclay Howell might have more on his mind than the next round of events at Baron's Hill, she thought ruefully. Of course, it was just as well that he hadn't asked her out. Attractive though he was, dating the boss was never a good idea. Too many things could go wrong.

But she couldn't deny that there was a flicker of disappointment deep inside her. Dana would have liked to get to know him better, to find out whether he really was as attractive as he seemed. If so, he might even be the one who could...

Then what he'd said hit her with the force of a hammer blow, and she sat up straight. "You mean Mr. Beeler isn't coming back after all? That was a particularly awful pneumonia, I know, but surely once he's completely over it, he'll be able to do his job again."

"He is recovering nicely, and he'll be back in a couple of weeks."

"Then— Oh, I see. It would probably be a good idea for him to have an assistant, at least for a while. That way he could stop when he was tired because I could take over, and—"

Barclay was smiling. "I don't intend for you to be his assistant, Dana, but his boss."

"You're demoting Mr. Beeler and putting me in his place? He isn't going to like that. He's been here forever, sir."

"He'll have the same position as always." Barclay sat down on the arm of a chair opposite Dana. "I'm not doing this very well, am I? Let me start over. Baron's Court will always need someone to manage all the official events that the president hosts, and Mr. Beeler fills that job very nicely."

"Then I don't see where I come in."

"He's very good with details, but Baron's Court needs more than that. It needs someone with vision and imagination and a sense of drama. It needs something that's been lacking ever since I took the job here. It needs..." He paused, as if he expected Dana to fill in the blank.

Dana stayed silent.

"It needs a hostess, Dana. The biggest difficulty about my position here has been trying to handle all the responsibilities alone.'' He chuckled. ''Not the professional ones, of course. But the social things—making nice with all the faculty spouses and the pennant-waving alumni... I'm certainly not fussing about those people, they're all quite charming really. But having someone to help with all that...''

''A hostess,'' Dana said slowly.

''Yes. You must have noticed how well we work together. We're a terrific team. And it would be quite a good opportunity for you. Though I wouldn't admit it publicly, of course, I don't intend to spend my whole career at a small private university. It's a good place for my first job in top administration, but I have my eye on something bigger. Much bigger.'' He sounded almost coy. ''You wouldn't lose by throwing in your lot with me.''

The ticklish feeling in Dana's stomach had turned into an actual pain. He couldn't possibly be saying what it sounded like. Teaming up with him...moving on to a bigger university...being his hostess... It sounded as if the man was talking about her whole life, not just a job.

No, she told herself, she was reading meanings where none existed. He couldn't possibly mean *that*.

A wicked little imp at the back of her brain made her wonder what he'd do if she threw herself at him and accepted a proposal he hadn't made. Watching the always-cool Barclay Howell turn pale and stammer in shock might be entertaining—and it would make him speak more carefully next time, too, instead of dancing around a subject like a politician. But it would hardly be a nice thing to do.

Barclay's smile began to look a little forced. "Dana, I'm asking you to marry me."

He was serious? She'd actually been right? She spoke before she stopped to think. "That's ridiculous. We've never even been to a movie together."

He frowned. "What does that have to do with it?"

The frightening thing, Dana thought, was that as far as he was concerned it wasn't a rhetorical question. Things like movies, dinners, walks in the park, getting to know each other...all were unimportant. Barclay Howell had made up his mind.

"I told you, we're an excellent team."

Funny, I thought proposals were supposed to cover things like love. "Sir, I think it would be best if—"

"Please, my dear. Call me Barclay. Since we're going to be married—"

Just a few minutes ago, she'd thought it was kind of cute how easily he could manipulate people into doing what he wanted. But now that he was using the knack to try to maneuver her, Dana was feeling something close to panic. "I haven't agreed to anything of the sort."

For one unguarded instant he looked startled by the possibility that she would consider turning him down, and then he smiled again. "Well, not yet," he said affably. "I suppose I was a bit abrupt."

A bit abrupt? That was one way to put it, Dana thought, though it wouldn't have been her first choice of words. The arrogance he was displaying was unbelievable, completely unlike the man she had thought he was.

So much for your judgment, she told herself. *But then, we've always known you weren't too sharp where men are concerned.*

"So I won't ask you for an answer just now. Take your time, and let me know when you're ready, Dana."

As if there could only be one answer. As if she was only delaying just so she didn't look desperate by snatching at his proposal...

Now she knew what Mrs. Janowitz had been talking about, when Dana had said she'd be going back to her regular job. *Of course that's the official line, for now. But those of us who can see what's really going on approve.*

The woman had known what Barclay Howell intended—long before Dana herself had even suspected. Had he taken a poll, for heaven's sake? Checked out his little idea with his advisers to make sure they wouldn't object to his choice of a first lady for the university?

It was just as well he wasn't demanding an answer right now. She'd have a hard time finding one that wouldn't singe Barclay Howell's aristocratic ears.

She got to her feet, feeling a little unsteady.

"Dana," he said. "Just one more thing before you go. I haven't had a chance to tell you how very important this cocktail party is. Quite possibly the most important one yet."

Dana was relieved to step back onto familiar ground, even though it seemed to be wobbling under her toes. The most important cocktail party yet? Why?

You should be honored, the imp at the back of her brain suggested, *that he proposed* before *he brought up the cocktail party.*

Dana ran through the guest list in her mind. The president's cocktail party was a regular monthly event, and tonight's guests were the usual mix. There were a few people from the foundation which raised funds for the university, a few of their most regular donors, a few alumni who might become donors, a few professors, and a few students being honored for special achievements. Dana couldn't think of anybody who was at all unusual. So what made this particular party any different than the one she'd arranged last month?

"I've invited an extra guest," Barclay said. "I happened to hear just this morning that he was in town, and I called him up on the chance that he might be free this evening. He seemed quite pleased to be asked. So I'd like you to make a special effort to make sure he feels welcome here."

Lingering shock made her feel like saying she'd tell the bartender to be sure the special guest got an extra paper umbrella in his drink, but she restrained herself. ''I try to arrange things so everyone feels welcome.''

''No, I mean a little personal effort. Instead of vanishing into the background tonight, Dana, I'd like you to stick around.''

''Play hostess,'' she said. The words tasted like sawdust.

''If you want to call it that. I'd rather think that you were trying out the role.''

''Whatever you wish, sir.''

He shook a gently chiding finger. ''You must get over that habit, my dear. When we're married…yes, I know, you haven't given me an answer yet. But you may as well get used to the change, anyway.''

Dana took a deep breath, decided not to say what she was thinking, and started for the door.

''Don't you want to know who the guest is?''

''It won't make any difference in how I treat him,'' Dana pointed out.

''Of course it won't, my dear.'' He started flipping through CDs again. ''Still, I think you should know. He might be the biggest single donor this university ever snags—he'll certainly have the cash to do it, when the sale of his company is final. And he owes us a debt of gratitude, too, since he got his degree here and that's what made him the success he is today. I looked it up, so I'd be sure to have it right—he studied mechanical engineering.''

Dana's breath caught in her throat.

Don't be silly, she told herself. Barclay hadn't given any time period; the man he was talking about might have graduated decades ago. If he was selling a company, he was probably near retirement age.

To say nothing of the fact that every semester there were at least a hundred graduates who'd majored in mechanical engineering, and a fair number of them must have eventually gone on to own good-size businesses. So why should her mind instantly conjure up a particular one? Especially when the one she was thinking of had said, the last time she'd talked to him, that he'd never set foot on this campus again.

Besides, there was absolutely no reason for her heart to start pounding like an out-of-

balance washing machine at the very thought
of him. That was over. Done with. Finished.

She managed a casual tone. ''So who is this
marvelous catch?''

Barclay said the name slowly, with relish,
as if the syllables tasted good. ''Zeke Ferris.''

And suddenly Dana's heart wasn't thumping
madly anymore. But that was only because it
had almost stopped beating altogether.

The foundation people were always the first to
arrive at any university function, because they
never missed an opportunity to talk someone
into making a pledge. Next came the honor
students, starched and stiff and on their best
behavior, sitting in a row along the edge of the
room. The professors always came as late as
they dared—missing the president's parties altogether would be extremely bad form, but a
token appearance was all that most of them
seemed to be able to stomach. The alumni and
the big donors trickled in and out throughout
the party, making it clear that they couldn't be
expected to limit themselves to one event per
evening.

But halfway through the time set aside for the cocktail party, it appeared that Zeke Ferris wasn't going to show up at all.

Dana circulated through the crowd, a half-full glass of sparkling water in her hand, making sure that no one was left out of the conversation. Some of the students looked as though they'd rather climb under their chairs than talk to the president.

Dana sympathized; she was feeling a bit out of place herself. Always before, she'd stayed in the shadows, orchestrating the party and keeping it running smoothly but not coming into direct contact with the guests. This, she thought irritably, would have to be the one evening that Barclay Howell changed the rules. She tried once more to smooth the creases out of her rust-colored skirt. She'd chosen the suit because it was just a shade darker than the auburn of her hair, and normally she liked wearing it. But tonight, next to the neat little cocktail dresses the other women were wearing, her suit felt sadly lacking in style. If she'd had any idea what Barclay had had in mind, she'd have brought along a change of clothes.

Beneath the president's smile, Dana could see tension. He kept looking toward the door—expectantly at first, then hopefully, and finally with irritation.

Dana was sorry for his disappointment, as well as relieved that Zeke hadn't shown up after all. But she was not at all surprised. Once she'd had a chance to calm down and think it over, she'd have been willing to bet her next paycheck that he wouldn't appear.

She entertained herself, while she pretended to listen to an alumni who wanted to describe in detail the last football game of his college career, by listing the possible reasons why Zeke wasn't there. First and most likely, Zeke had accepted the invitation and then completely forgotten the time and even the day. Or perhaps he had actually not accepted the invitation at all, but Barclay thought he had. *The same way he thinks I've accepted his proposal,* Dana thought. Or, possibly, Zeke had never intended to show up—though he wasn't habitually rude. At least, he hadn't been when....

But she wasn't going to think about that.

That's over, she reminded herself. *Done with. Finished.*

Just as the alumnus was reaching the climactic play of the game he was describing, gesturing wildly as he demonstrated the gymnastics required to cross the goal line, the chatter of the crowd dropped by a good ten decibels. Sensitive to the atmosphere of the party, Dana let her gaze sweep across the room, seeking out the cause of the sudden comparative silence.

Not that it required much effort. Her attention, like that of every other person in the room, was drawn as if by a magnet to a man standing in the arched doorway between the drawing room and the entrance hall. He was tall and lean, dressed in a silvery-gray business suit, and he stood perfectly at ease as he surveyed the room. His face was shadowed by the deep arch, but the light of the chandelier behind him fell warmly across his black hair, almost crowning him with its golden glow.

Like he's wearing a halo, Dana thought grimly. *I've never seen a better example of false advertising.*

She surveyed the perfect tailoring of his suit with interest and had to admit a wisp of relief that he hadn't shown up in blue jeans and a flannel shirt. Not that it mattered to her what

he wore, she added hastily. Or how he presented himself to a crowd.

Barclay had hurried toward him, beaming,
his hand extended. "Mr. Ferris," he ex-
claimed. "How kind of you to honor us with
your presence tonight. I hope your business
meetings went well today."

Zeke stepped forward. The halo vanished as
the soft light of the drawing room fell across
his face. "Call me Zeke," Dana heard him
say.

The alumnus cleared his throat, and she
turned hastily back to him. "And that was the
play which won the game?"

But the man wasn't looking at her. He was
staring at Zeke. "What's so important about
that young fella?" he demanded. "President's
hardly said a word to me all evening, but he
falls all over him. Has he given a lot of money
to the university, or something?"

"Not yet," Dana said.

"Oh, I see. Howell's trying to put the
squeeze on him. Well, I suppose there's never
enough money."

A man on Dana's other side, a member of
the university's board of directors, said, "You

can say that again. We need a new stadium, for one thing.''

Dana started to say that the last thing Zeke Ferris was likely to give the university was a sports stadium, but she stopped herself just in time. How could she know that, anyway? People changed—the Zeke Ferris she had known certainly hadn't been the perfectly-tailored business suit type. ''And we could use a new conference center,'' she pointed out.

''Oh, well, I suppose if you're interested in that sort of thing,'' one of the men conceded.

She left the two of them discussing the university's sports program and excused herself. But the party seemed to be taking care of itself at the moment; no one was standing alone, no one was looking forlorn, and no one seemed to be plunging into an argument. When a waiter passed, she swapped her sparkling water for a glass of champagne, and as she turned away she came face-to-face with Zeke Ferris.

She looked past him and saw that the alumnus who had told her all about the game he'd won had buttonholed Barclay as he crossed the room and was drawing him off into a corner. Even Barclay's celebrated people skills might

not get him out of that conversation in a hurry,
she thought.

She'd almost forgotten how tall Zeke was.
Even in her highest heels she'd always had to
look up at him. Today, in the comfortable flats
she habitually wore when she was in charge of
a party, she seemed to look a very long way
up into eyes bright as sapphires and filled with
speculation.

"Dana," he said softly. "Now this is a surprise."

He had not said, she noted, that it was a
pleasant surprise. *And you can multiply that
reaction times two,* she thought. But she
smiled and put out her hand. "Zeke."

His grip was warm and firm, and he contin-
ued to hold her hand. "It's been a long time."

Not long enough.

He looked around the room and then back
at her. "So what are you doing here?" he
asked. "Are you faculty? Staff? Or are you
finally going after that graduate degree you
wanted so badly?"

"Staff," she said coolly, and tugged her
hand away. He let her fingers slip slowly out
of his. She could feel her hands trembling, so
she folded both of them around her cold glass

to hide the telltale tremor. "I hope you'll enjoy your visit here, Zeke. May I get you a drink?"

She watched a smile tug at the corner of his mouth. He might as well have said it, she thought, for it was quite clear what he was thinking. *So that's the way you're going to play it.*

"When you said you were staff," Zeke murmured, "I thought you meant something administrative. It didn't occur to me you might be just a waitress."

Dana gritted her teeth. *He's trying to jab you into making a scene,* she told herself.

Behind her, Barclay said smoothly, "I'm sure you misunderstood, Zeke."

Dana had no trouble interpreting his tone of voice. No matter what a prospective donor said, it wasn't to be taken as an insult—it was merely a misunderstanding.

"This is Dana Mulholland," Barclay went on. "She's not a waitress, she manages all the conferences and special events that the university hosts, and she's been filling in at Baron's Hill as well. In fact—"

Dana stepped quickly into the gap. "When we finish raising the money to build a new conference center, I'll be in charge of it."

"That's not what I meant, my dear, but I know you're right. Since it's not quite official yet, I probably shouldn't say anything at all. But it's so hard to keep such happy news a secret." Barclay's tone was confidential, almost intimate.

Zeke's eyes had narrowed, and only then did Dana realize that Barclay had draped an arm around her shoulders. She tried to shrug it off.

Barclay's grip tightened. "I've asked Dana to marry me."

Dana wanted to stuff her fingers in her ears on the theory that if she couldn't hear what was going on, then it wasn't really happening.

A member of the board of directors, standing nearby, cocked his head to one side. "Did I hear you right, Howell?" he asked. "You're marrying Dana?"

"I wasn't actually going to announce it just yet," Barclay began.

He's keeping his options open, Dana deduced.

But the director didn't pause. "Capital idea. I don't mind telling you there was some hesitation on the part of the board when we hired you. We wondered if putting a young man, a bachelor, in that position was just asking for trouble. But marrying Dana—now that's sensible. Like you're taking the university to your bosom, eh? Making it your own.'' He chortled at his own wit.

Dana's face felt hot. *Say something,* she ordered herself. *Deny it—and fast.*

But that would mean contradicting Barclay in public and mortifying him in front of directors and alumni and faculty. Not that he didn't deserve it—but if nothing else, self-preservation suggested she keep quiet for the moment and deal with the proposal later, when she could be alone with Barclay. Embarrassing the president of the university wasn't the best way to improve her job security.

And why should she provide any more of a scene for Zeke Ferris's entertainment, anyway? It was none of his business what she did.

''And marriage will help keep all the other women from circling around, too,'' an alumnus added. ''You must have been having to beat them off with a baseball bat this last year.''

Barclay's self-deprecating smile and vague gesture of denial were so halfhearted, Dana thought, that he might as well have come straight out and said yes, the women found him so attractive that he was forced to defend himself.

The sheer arrogance of the man made Dana seethe with fury. She was drawing breath to set the record straight when she caught a glimpse of Zeke's face. She blinked in astonishment. She hadn't expected that he'd rush to congratulate them—but she also hadn't expected to see pity in his eyes. Pity? How dare he pity her?

He looked at her levelly for a long moment. "Now that could present a problem," he said finally. "Because she can't."

Dana's temper snapped. Even though she had no intention of marrying Barclay Howell, the very idea of Zeke telling her she couldn't was enough to make her spit nails. "Oh, for heaven's sake, Zeke, don't try to lay down the law to me. There is absolutely no reason for you to have an opinion in the matter. Whether I get married or not has nothing to do with you."

"Much as I hate to disagree with a lady—"

"You expect me to believe *that* piece of nonsense?"

He wasn't looking at her, but at Barclay. "She can't get married till her divorce is final."

"Divorce?" Barclay said blankly.

Dana's jaw dropped. "*What?* We took care of that years ago. You have absolutely no claim on me anymore, Zeke, so stop acting like a dog in the manger."

"You're divorced?" Barclay sounded as if he was about to faint.

"That's the problem," Zeke murmured. "She isn't, actually. There was a little hangup with the paperwork, and so our divorce never quite went through. Sorry to break the news this way, darling—but you're still married. To me."

CHAPTER TWO

THE room seemed to whirl around Dana.

It wasn't possible, she thought. It was six years since they'd called it quits, and the proof was buried at the back of the fire-safe box in her closet where she kept her most important papers.

Or...was it?

Suddenly—illogically—doubt swept over her. She had certainly received documents. But when that long brown envelope had finally arrived, months after they'd actually split, she'd simply glanced at the papers inside before she'd put the package away. Half of her had been relieved that the whole mess was over, but the other half was still stinging with misery and injured pride. The last thing she'd wanted to do was read every last detail, set down in harsh black and white in a chilly legal document, concerning the most painful mistake of her life.

But she'd looked at it closely enough to know what it was—a final dissolution of her brief marriage. Zeke was wrong, that was all there was to it. Where he'd gotten the idea that the divorce hadn't gone through was beyond her, but he had to be wrong.

Or else he was flat-out lying.

She found herself looking uncertainly at him. The one thing he had never done, in their months together, was to lie to her.

People change, she thought. But did they change in such essential ways as that?

Of course, the fact that he'd never lied to her wasn't exactly an accolade, Dana told herself. There had been times during their brief marriage when Zeke's bluntness had not helped the situation at all. For instance, during that last argument when he'd made it clear that he was anxious not only to get away from the campus but from her...

This is no time to be reliving the past, she reminded herself. *You've got enough to deal with right now.* Like the fact that Barclay's face had turned purple and he looked as if he couldn't breathe.

She hit him a sharp blow between the shoulder blades, just in case he'd inhaled an olive, and he gasped, choked, and started to laugh. ''For a minute there, I thought you were serious," he said. "What a joker—I'd heard you have quite a sense of humor, Zeke, but I had no idea it was quite so...unusual."

Zeke looked down at him, eyes half-hooded. Though he was only a couple of inches taller than Barclay, somehow he managed to make it look like much more, as though he towered over the other man.

It was a good trick, Dana thought. Under other circumstances, she might have been amused at his lord-of-the-manor pose.

"Oh, it's a side-splitter of a story, all right," Zeke said agreeably. "I'm glad you enjoyed my efforts to entertain you, Bark."

If he hadn't already had a shock, Dana suspected Barclay wouldn't even have winced at the mangling of his name. But obviously he wasn't fully recovered yet, for distaste flickered across his face. "Uh...yeah," he said. "Let me get you that drink Dana promised you."

He strode off toward the bar. The buzz of conversation picked up again, and for a moment Zeke and Dana were almost alone in the center of the room.

"I don't know what game you're playing," Dana said, "but I don't appreciate it."

"Sorry to interrupt your life, honey, but it isn't a game." Zeke's gaze shifted to a point over her shoulder.

Dana was furious. "You can't just come in here and make an announcement like that and then ignore me when I ask for an explanation!"

"Oh, you want an explanation," he said with a bright-eyed air of discovery. "And here I thought you'd already decided I'd made it up just to interfere in your new romance."

"As if you'd want to," Dana snapped.

He looked appraisingly at her. "Don't you mean, *'As if you could'*? Come between you and the new boyfriend, I mean."

"That, too." It came out sounding a little lame, Dana thought, but her feelings—or lack of them—for Barclay were certainly none of Zeke's business.

"Though I'd be doing you a favor if I did break it up. Honestly, Dana, can't you do any better than Barclay Howell?"

"Coming from you, Zeke, that's the funniest joke of the year."

"Everybody thinks I'm so humorous, maybe I should take up comedy."

"You'd fit right into the profession," Dana said coolly.

Zeke reached past her to take the glass Barclay was holding. "Thanks, Bark."

Dana bit her tongue. The night was young, and sooner or later she'd have a chance to get Zeke off in a corner and shake an explanation out of him. Whether he could adequately justify what he'd done was probably another question altogether, but at least she could find out what he'd been thinking when he made that bizarre announcement.

In the meantime, she decided, the best way to head off more questions was to pretend nothing important had happened. She smiled at Barclay. "You must ask Zeke to tell you about his first couple of years here. The university had quite a reputation as a party school back then, and he helped add a chapter to the story. If you'll excuse me, gentlemen, I see that Professor Wells has just arrived. I'm helping her to organize an event that's coming up later this week, and I must ask her about a few details." She tried not to give a sigh of relief as she made her escape.

Professor Wells was at the bar, taking a tentative sip of her Scotch and water. "I hate these parties," she grumbled to Dana. "But at least I'll say for Barclay Howell that he insists on good Scotch. I think the stuff the last president served was really antifreeze. How are the arrangements for the trivia tournament shaping up?"

Dana bit back a smile. "I'm sure the sponsors of the Academic Honors Bowl wouldn't like hearing you call it a trivia tournament."

"Then they should make it a real contest. Put in some questions that require intellect and reasoning instead of a command of random information."

"Finding enough dormitory space to house a couple of hundred high school students overnight wasn't easy," Dana admitted. "And I'm having a little trouble with the awards ceremony at the end of the day. The lecture hall in the conference center isn't large enough to hold all the students who are taking part, but I can't put chairs in the aisles or the fire inspector will have a fit."

Professor Wells grunted. "If enough of them get bored and leave early, there'll be no shortage of seats."

"That's true, but it's hardly the solution we want."

"I know, Dana. We really need that new building. Of course, don't hold your breath. If the trustees have their way, there'll be a new stadium first, and then a basketball arena, and then—"

Dana was having trouble concentrating. She realized suddenly that even with her back turned she knew exactly where in the room Zeke was at any given moment. The hairs at the nape of Dana's neck seemed to be acting as a sort of compass, with Zeke being true north. It didn't help that Barclay seemed to be showing him off, making the rounds of the room in order to introduce him to everyone.

She finally gave up on making sense of the conversation and told Professor Wells she'd phone her the next day to get the list of people who had volunteered to serve as question-readers and judges for the academic bowl. Instantly her internal radar seemed to relax a bit, but as soon as she turned her attention back to the room, she saw why.

Zeke was leaving. He was already in the entrance hall, with Barclay beside him, obviously almost pleading with him to stay a little longer. She watched as Zeke shook his head and went out.

He had been there less than half an hour, but that short space of time had thrown Dana into the worst emotional turmoil she'd felt since their divorce. And now he was escaping without giving her any justification at all for his behavior.

Which was pretty much par for the course where Zeke was concerned.

Barclay closed the door behind him and came straight across the drawing room to Dana. He looked, she thought warily, as if he'd like to kick the nearest alumnus. She braced herself. How was she going to explain that incredible announcement of Zeke's when she had no idea herself what he'd been talking about?

"You could have told me you knew him." It sounded like an accusation.

"There was no reason to. It was back in the dark ages."

"The timing doesn't matter."

"Look," she said, keeping her voice low. "You must realize you took me by surprise earlier this evening. If we'd been dating, of course I would have told you I'd been married before. But it's not something I announce when I'm first introduced to someone, so—"

Barclay waved a hand, dismissing her concern. "I wasn't talking about that."

Dana almost choked. "Then what are you talking about?"

"You could at least have filled me in about his history," he said impatiently. "Warned me about that kooky sense of humor...you mean you really were married to him?"

Dana nodded. "For about three months."

"Oh. Well, that's nothing."

Nothing, Dana thought. But did he mean that her short-lived marriage was unimportant because it had no implications for her current decisions, or because finding out about it had changed his mind about the offer he'd made?

Not that it altered her feelings about Barclay in the least, but it would be convenient to know whether she was still supposed to be considering his proposal. Why waste time trying to find a way to let him down gently, if he had decided she wasn't suitable marriage material after all?

Barclay sounded aggrieved. "You could at least have suggested the best way to approach him."

As if he were a rattlesnake, Dana thought. "You want my advice on how to get a donation out of Zeke Ferris? Sorry, but I have no idea how to persuade the man to part with his money, because when I knew him he didn't have any. I'm the one who paid for the divorce.''

The divorce I didn't get after all... She told herself firmly not to leap to conclusions. Just because Zeke had said something didn't make it true. Maybe Barclay was right, and Zeke had intended it as a sort of practical joke. Then, as soon as he'd realized that she didn't find it amusing, he'd sloped off rather than take responsibility for a gag gone bad...

But that behavior wasn't like the Zeke she'd known, either. Dana's head was starting to pound.

She had never in her life been so glad to see the end of a party. She pitched in to help the caterers clean up, partly so they could all go home sooner, partly because she didn't want to face another tête-á-tête with Barclay just now—but mostly because as long as she was surrounded by a group of outsiders, Connie couldn't ask her any questions. And since at the moment she had absolutely no answers...

She kept on working after Connie gave up and left. Finally, when the last members of the catering crew were ready to go, Dana took her raincoat from a hook near the kitchen door and went out with them. The last truck roared away and she was alone.

The dark and gloomy afternoon had given way to a darker and gloomier evening. It wasn't quite raining, but the air was so heavy with mist that the usual evening sounds were softened and flattened. Her footsteps on the brick driveway didn't make the usual sharp click, and the creak of the gate as she opened and closed it was unusually muted. The sound of a car engine starting might have come from any direction at all.

She turned toward downtown, to walk the dozen blocks to her little house. Her hands were deep in the pockets of her raincoat and her head was bent against the misty air. She was vaguely aware of a car coming up behind her, but that was nothing new. It would have been more unusual for the streets to be empty at this hour in this neighborhood. Though she felt dead tired, in fact it wasn't late.

It took her a while to realize that the car was moving too slowly. It should have passed her by now. Was it following her?

She shot a nervous glance over her shoulder and speeded her steps. A Jaguar. If a stalker was after her, she thought, at least he had good taste.

The car crept along beside her for another few yards, then pulled in toward the curb. The passenger-side window opened and a man leaned across the seat to look out at her.

''Want a lift?'' Zeke asked.

''I was enjoying my solitude,'' Dana pointed out. She kept walking.

The car crept along beside her. ''I thought you wanted an explanation.''

She stopped. ''Does that mean you're actually planning to give me one?''

''Get in.'' He pushed the door open.

She perched sideways on the seat with the door open and one foot still planted on the street.

''You never used to be the nervous sort,'' Zeke said, ''but at the moment you look like you're ready to run. And yet you're walking home at this hour. The two things don't fit together somehow.''

''Give it a little thought and I'm sure you can figure out why I'm a bit jittery at the idea of sitting here.'' Her voice was dry. ''What gives, Zeke?''

''I wouldn't want you to be uncomfortable. If you don't want to sit here, let's go somewhere for dinner.''

''Let's have that explanation first.''

''I'm too hungry to keep my mind on details.''

''It's your own fault if you're hungry. There was food at the party.''

''That's what you call food? Those dainty little nibbles didn't even take the edge off. I've been sitting here fantasizing about a steak. I had just about convinced myself I was wasting my time waiting for you to come out. Another five minutes and I'd have been gone.''

''My timing always was rotten,'' Dana murmured. ''So if you were going to wait five more minutes for me anyway, you might as well put it to good use. Give me the condensed version and then you can go eat. And by the way, if that remark about wasting your time waiting for me was a polite way of asking whether I've moved in with Barclay, the answer is no.''

"Oh, I'm sure you still go home every night…eventually. Barclay wouldn't want any gossip about his future wife."

Dana hit her temple with the heel of her hand. "What on earth is wrong with me? Did I just imply that you were trying to be polite? My mistake. I take it all back." She slid out of the car, slammed the door, and leaned in the still-open window. "If you waited around just so you could insult me, you wasted your time, Zeke. Good night." She took two steps.

The car crept forward. "You keep saying you want me to tell you what happened."

"Well—yes, now that you mention it, it would be nice to know what inspired you to say such a stupid thing. No, wait—let me guess. You just had to make sure that Barclay knew I'd been married—is that it?"

Zeke's voice was soft. "So I was right on target. You hadn't told him."

Dana could have kicked herself for admitting as much. "No, I hadn't. But—" She stopped. She was not about to confide in Zeke that she hadn't even known Barclay well enough to tell him about her past; Zeke would laugh himself into tears.

"Barclay's first lady will have to be like Caesar's wife, you know," he said with a sanctimonious air that made Dana want to punch him. "He couldn't possibly marry any woman who had a breath of suspicion hanging over her, and I...well, I just couldn't live with myself if I hadn't done my best to prevent a scandal."

"You're the one who *caused* the scandal," Dana pointed out. "Besides, there's nothing for anyone to be scandalized about. It happens all the time. We got married, we decided it didn't work, we got divorced—"

Zeke shook his head. "Not quite."

"Look, enough of the joke already."

"I wish it was a joke, Dana."

There was a deep and obviously heartfelt note in his voice that made Dana's stomach feel like lead. She said uncertainly, "You weren't making it up?"

Zeke shook his head. "Come on," he said and pushed the car door open. "We've got some talking to do."

Dana chose the restaurant, but as soon as they walked in Zeke knew why she'd made that particular selection—it was the darkest little bar he'd ever been in. "I can't quite see Barclay bringing you here," he murmured as she led the way to a table. "As a matter of fact, I can't see much of anything at all. But I suppose that's the biggest attraction of the place—he's not likely to walk in and spot us together."

To his disappointment Dana didn't rise to the bait. "No, I chose it because the music is loud enough to keep anyone from overhearing us, but not so loud that we'll have to shout. And you did say you wanted a steak—they're supposed to have the best ones in town."

"Supposed to? You don't know? Don't tell me you've gone vegetarian." She looked it, he thought. She was thinner than he remembered. Did that mean that Barclay liked his women as angular as clothing racks?

"I got so used to rice and beans when we were married that it became a habit."

"Sarcasm isn't your strong point, Dana."

"Then I'll have to work harder at it." She took a menu from behind the salt and pepper shakers and handed it to him. It was so battered that the lamination was coming loose from the paper. Zeke maneuvered the menu into the glow of the single narrow spotlight above the table and tried to read around the scratches and reflections.

Dana seemed to have no trouble figuring out what the menu said. "It's my lucky day," she said. "Pinto bean and wild rice soup. Just what I wanted."

"Don't starve yourself for my sake."

"Still being bossy, I see." She put her menu down with a slap.

"No, just practical. I saw you knocking back champagne at Barclay's party, and if we're going to have a serious discussion—"

"You'd like me to be sober for it? Gee, and here I thought you were asking me out to dinner for old times' sake. You can rest easy, Zeke. I had one glass of champagne. I carried it around with me most of the evening, and I dumped the last of it down the drain right before I left Baron's Hill."

"Fine." One thing was already obvious, Zeke thought. She was still just as stubborn as she'd ever been—if not more so.

"But if you insist, I'll order something besides rice and bean soup." She looked up at the server. "I'll have your most expensive steak." She pointed at Zeke. "And he'll have the bill."

The server didn't even blink. "For you, sir?"

"Make it two." The server went away, and Zeke said, "The last thing I would have expected, years ago when we were just trying to survive the semester, was that you'd end up being the university's first lady."

Dana shrugged and fiddled with her menu, putting it neatly back in place and propping it up with the ketchup bottle. "And who would have thought you'd end up as Mr. Industrialist?"

"Not for much longer."

She nodded. "Barclay said something about you selling your business. He's hoping that when you hold all those millions in your hands, you'll remember the university with fondness."

"Tell me something I didn't know," Zeke said dryly.

"What are you going to do then? Go lie on a beach in Hawaii?"

Zeke shook his head. "Oh, no. I wouldn't dream of restricting myself to one beach when there must be hundreds of them out there around the world, just waiting for me."

Her laugh brought a sparkle of gold to her big brown eyes, he noted. At least that much hadn't changed.

The server brought salads and a basket of bread.

Dana drizzled blue cheese dressing over her lettuce. "All right," she said. "Enough polite conversation. What makes you think—"

"Poor Barclay," Zeke interrupted.

Dana paused. "What about him?" She sounded a little uncertain.

"He must think you're a diplomat, or he wouldn't have proposed. Boy, is he in for a nasty shock."

"Thank you very much for that helpful dissection of my character. I don't normally have trouble making nice to people—only when they say completely idiotic things. What makes you so sure there's something wrong with the divorce, anyway? I have all the papers—or didn't the lawyer ever send you a set?" Her eyes widened. "Dammit, Zeke, if you caused all this trouble just because you didn't get any paperwork—"

"I got it. It's a very impressive set of documents. Lots of fine print and gold seals and

flowery signatures and whereases and hereto-
fores.''

''Yeah,'' Dana said slowly, ''that sounds
like the same thing I got. But then—''

''Did you ever read the fine print?''

She hesitated, as if she was considering the
ramifications of telling the truth, before she finally said, ''No. Not all of it.''

''Well, I didn't either, until just recently. It
turns out that we applied for a divorce in the
Dominican Republic instead of Wisconsin. Or,
rather, our attorney applied, in our names.''

Dana looked at him blankly. ''Why would
he do such a thing?''

''Apparently because he'd found it to be a
very accommodating legal system—and it ap-
pears to be a perfectly fine one for the people
who live there. Unfortunately, as far as I can
find out, very few other courts in the world
seems to recognize a Dominican divorce as legal. So if a couple who lives in Wisconsin gets
a divorce in the—''

''They're not really divorced at all,'' Dana
groaned.

''Not unless they move to the Caribbean.
Though, come to think of it, there are plenty
of beaches there. It's worth considering.''

She obviously wasn't listening. "That shyster! Why bother to file it anywhere? Why not just create the fancy document out of thin air and tell us it was real? We'd have believed it— we'd have believed anything he told us. We were just a couple of kids who were anxious to put a mistake behind us."

"I suppose he thought that making it up out of whole cloth would be unethical."

"Unethical!" She made a noise that sounded like a snort. "It sounds to me as if he wouldn't know an ethic if it bit him in the nose."

Pure mischief made him say, "You have to give him a little credit for having a conscience. The document we got is certainly real, even if it doesn't exactly accomplish what we intended it to."

"Cut it out, Zeke. The man was only after the money, and you know it. He probably calculated the cost of every last gold seal."

"The question now, of course, is what we're going to do about it."

"That's a no-brainer," Dana said promptly. "We hire another attorney and get a real divorce this time. No, on second thought, the first thing I want to do is sue him to get my money back, and then—''

Zeke frowned. What was she talking about? ''Get your money back?''

''Yes.'' She thrust out her chin. ''As long as we're hashing out leftover details, that's another thing we might as well talk about. I know you were strapped for cash at the time, but so was I. That was why we agreed to cooperate instead of hiring two attorneys in the first place.''

''That was your brilliant idea, I believe,'' he murmured. ''And an expensive mistake it turned out to be.''

She glowered at him. ''I'm not the only one he fooled. And stop trying to change the subject. I didn't appreciate you sticking me with the bill for the divorce, Zeke. Splitting it down the middle would have been fair, but saddling me with the whole thing—''

No wonder she wants her money back. ''I didn't do anything of the sort,'' Zeke said.

''Don't try to weasel out of it now, because it can't be done. Not only did I pay the whole bill, but I kept the cancelled checks as a reminder to be more careful who I got involved with next time.''

He didn't doubt it for a minute. Not that the resolution appeared to have done her much good—taking up with Barclay Howell, for heaven's sake. What was the woman thinking of?

He spoke slowly and deliberately. "So did I, Dana."

She stared at him. "You...what?"

Zeke said gently, "I paid the whole bill." He watched her face turn pale under the brilliant spotlight as comprehension slowly dawned.

"He charged us both? And all this time I was thinking that you'd ducked out of paying your share." Her voice cracked. "And you thought I'd dodged mine."

"No, I just believed it was my responsibility, so I took care of it."

She swallowed hard, but she obviously wasn't in the mood to give him points for acting like a gentleman. "That *shark*." She stretched out her hands, fingers spread like claws. "When I get hold of him—"

She wasn't wearing an engagement ring, Zeke noted absently. She wasn't wearing any jewelry at all, in fact; not only were her hands bare but her neck was unadorned as well. Pity, he thought. It was a neck that was made for delicate gold chains. Her throat was slim and long, with an aristocratic arch. It had always been a very kissable little neck. He wondered if Barclay had discovered the ticklish spot right below her ear....

None of your business, Ferris.

''I wouldn't recommend it,'' he said mildly. ''You'd be bound to be caught if you committed assault and battery inside a federal penitentiary, and Barclay might not like it.''

''Our attorney is in a federal prison?''

Zeke nodded. ''He's already served two years of an eight-to-ten for fraud.''

''So that's how you found out we're not divorced after all? A story in the newspaper or something.''

He toyed with the idea of simply nodding. It would certainly be the easiest course. But Dana had already proved that she wasn't going to be easily convinced, and he wouldn't put it past her to demand that he produce the newspaper clipping. The trouble was that there had been no news coverage—or at least none that he'd seen.

''Not exactly,'' he said. ''Arranging faulty divorces isn't what he's in prison for. As a matter of fact, I didn't know he was in prison till I tried to look him up so he could explain how the hell he'd messed up ours. Until then, I thought it was just a simple mistake.''

The server returned with two platters topped with still-sizzling steaks. Good timing, Zeke thought, and changed the subject. ''How long have you known Barclay?''

Dana paid no attention to either her plate or his question. ''How did you find out there was anything wrong?''

He met her gaze, levelly. ''I happened to run across the divorce papers one day and I decided to check everything out and make sure it was all in order.''

Her eyes narrowed. ''Six years after the fact, you just took it into your head to ask an attorney whether you were really divorced?''

''Call it a whim. And it turned out to be a sensible one, too.''

She looked at him for a long moment and then shook her head. ''Oh, no, you don't, Zeke. You're not going to make me believe that you had nothing better to do than run down the details of a six-year-old legal case. Or to pay a lawyer to do it, either. So what's really going on?''

He cut a slice from his steak. "This will lose half its flavor if you let it get cold," he warned.

Dana didn't seem to hear him. "I've got it. You're planning a little walk down the aisle yourself. And your new bride—who must be a more careful sort than I ever was—wanted to be certain you were really and truly free."

"Nice story. Not a word of truth in it, but you get credit for a noble effort."

"Oh, come on. Why should I care that you're planning to get married? You can tell me all about her. Maybe I'll invite her to lunch someday—give her some pointers about handling you. She might even ask me to be a bridesmaid." Dana started to laugh. "If you could see your face, Zeke... You're acting as if you think I'm going to refuse to divorce you this time around." She stopped dead, staring at him.

He watched her with interest. The play of emotion across her face was fascinating—first laughter, then shock, and then the beginnings of grim anger.

"You *do*," she accused. "You are actually arrogant enough to think I'm going to stand in your way. As if I'd be stupid enough to want you back! I couldn't wait to get out of our marriage last time around, and I'm certainly not going to hold you up...''

Zeke cut another bite of his steak and waited patiently for her to run down.

''Hold you up,'' she repeated. ''I get it now. Last time neither of us had a dime, so there was no problem about who got what. But now you're sitting on a gold mine—and you think I'm mercenary enough to want to stay married to you just so I can help spend it.''

''If that was what I thought, Dana, I would just have waited to tell you about the divorce till the business was sold.''

Dana shook her head. ''No, you wouldn't— because then you'd have cash in your hands. I could demand part of that in return for your freedom. Well, let me assure you I won't. I want to be free just as much as you do, and it can't happen soon enough for me.''

Here's your chance, Ferris. Make it good.

''Now that is a difficulty,'' Zeke said calmly. ''Because you see, Dana...I don't.''

CHAPTER THREE

DANA pushed her plate away and propped both elbows on the table, steadying her chin in her hands while she tried to decide whether Zeke could have possibly said what she thought she'd heard. He couldn't have, she decided. She must have been hallucinating, because he didn't seem to realize he had said anything unusual at all. And he certainly wasn't waiting for a reaction, the way he would if he'd deliberately thrown out a bombshell like that one; he was concentrating on his steak as if it was the only important issue in his life at the moment.

It was an odd thing for her to hallucinate about, though. Out of the blue, to imagine that Zeke wanted her back... She wasn't even in the habit of thinking about him. Not often, anyway. She must have been even more shaken than she'd realized by his announcement—and that was saying something.

"In case I didn't make myself quite clear," Zeke said finally, "I mean that I don't want a divorce."

Dana supposed that announcement should make her feel better, because there was no question this time what he'd meant, and that proved she wasn't hearing odd voices in her head after all. Unfortunately, establishing that she wasn't the crazy one didn't eliminate the problem.

"Well, you always were a little irrational about certain subjects," she said, trying to sound calm. "But this confirms it—you've lost your ever-lovin' mind. Of course you want a divorce, Zeke. You've *had* a divorce for the past six years." She saw him start to shake his head and rolled her eyes. "So all right, maybe it wasn't quite legal—but we thought it was. We both lived as if we were single. You absolutely cannot expect me to believe that you've gone around for the last six years regretting our breakup and living like a monk while you tried to figure out a way to get me back."

"No," Zeke said.

"Good. At least you know better than to insult my intelligence. So what on earth do you mean, you don't want a divorce?"

"Not at the moment anyway."

"At the moment? Okay, I'll wait five minutes and try again." She pulled her plate back and cut into her steak. "In the meantime—"

"And not for the next few months. About three should do it, I think."

Dana put down her fork. "I'm not even going to ask you to explain the logic behind that. But I don't see the problem. If we'd file the papers tomorrow, it would take at least that long before the divorce is final and you're free. Even if the court rushed everything through, three months from now we'll still be married..." Her voice trailed off. "I can't believe I'm actually saying that."

"But as soon as we asked for a divorce, it would be clear that I was going to be unattached within a relatively short space of time."

"And you don't want to be free?"

"Ultimately, yes. Of course I do. But not for the next three months."

"What's magical about three months, for heaven's sake?"

"I thought you weren't going to ask me to explain." He held up both hands, palms out. "Okay, okay—no more teasing. I haven't forgotten the symptoms when you're about to blow up."

"Good for you," Dana muttered.

Zeke tipped his water glass and used the edge of the heavy base to draw invisible circles on the tabletop. "You said Barclay told you I'm selling my company."

Dana nodded.

"Well, he's a little ahead of the times. I'm negotiating a sale, but it isn't final yet."

"No wonder you weren't eager to write the university a check."

"And I never will be as long as he's in charge."

"Tell me, Zeke..." Dana's voice dripped irony. "Exactly when did you acquire this overwhelming fondness for Barclay? Because if I didn't know better, I'd say you were acting jealous."

"Oh, absolutely," Zeke said lightly. "I've been watching you from afar these last six years and setting private detectives to check out every guy you dated. I can tell you exactly how many times you've been kissed good night at the front door.''

Dana didn't believe him for an instant. ''Only at the front door? Surely you didn't neglect to bug my bedroom.''

''Dana!'' He sounded shocked. ''There are some things a gentleman just won't do.''

''Right. I'd put more stock in that if you behaved like a gentleman even when it wasn't convenient. It's interesting that all through these years of spying on me, this is the first time you felt it necessary to intervene in my private life. I suppose you're going to tell me that your Don Quixote impulses got the best of you?''

''And sent me rushing to rescue you from Barclay,'' he agreed. ''I find it fascinating, of course, that you seem to think you need rescuing... Was that one of those nasty Freudian slips, my dear?''

Dana bit her tongue. When was she going to learn to watch every word she said? He'd always been deadly in an argument. ''Let's leave Barclay out of it, all right?''

Zeke shrugged. ''Fine, just remember that you're the one who brought him in. But let me put your mind at rest on the jealousy question.

I disliked Barclay the moment I heard his unctuous, oily voice on the telephone.''

''Then—if you were so unimpressed with him—why did you accept his invitation to the cocktail party?''

''Because I was looking for you, sweetheart, and I thought if he called the alumni office to vouch for me, I'd have an easier time of getting your current address.''

''Why didn't you just ask all your private investigators where to find me?'' Dana asked sweetly.

Zeke had gone straight on. ''I didn't expect to run into you right at Barclay's elbow.'' He raised his eyebrows. ''Come to think of it, why *were* you at Barclay's elbow? And don't give me the obvious answer, because I'm not asking what you see in him. I want to know why you're even at the university. You were as anxious to shake the dust of this town off your feet as I was.''

''No—I was anxious to get out of the marriage. I'm here because I was offered a very good job, with a lot of potential for advancement.''

Zeke shrugged. ''I guess, if marrying Barclay is your idea of advancing...''

"That isn't what I was talking about. I was hired to promote the idea of a conference center, to develop the plans and create demand for the facility. In another year or two, when it's completed, I'll be in charge of a brand-new, state-of-the-art building and all the business that goes with it. The university will be the place to go for conventions, parties, product launches, weddings—"

"And in the meantime?"

She admitted, reluctantly, "We're located in Dressler Hall."

"Refresh my memory. Is that the building on the corner of the quadrangle, the one that's all falling plaster and bats?"

"Not anymore. Stop changing the subject, Zeke. You still haven't told me why you want to be unavailable for the next three months, much less why you want to look as if you're going to be unavailable forever. You'll notice I didn't assume that you actually want to be married to *me*."

"Smart girl," Zeke said. "To put it in a nutshell, the corporation that wants to buy my business has indicated that they want me to be part of the package."

"Work for them, you mean? It's not exactly unusual."

"The CEO is quite insistent."

"So tell him you've done all the work you intend to in this lifetime and you're going to lie on a beach for the next forty years. I don't see why you think being married will solve that problem."

"The female CEO."

Dana shredded a bit of steak while she thought about it. "And the package she wants to buy includes you personally? Isn't that called sexual harassment?"

"Try to prove it. Besides, she's far too subtle to say it directly. That's part of the problem—if she'd come out in the open, I could deflect her, but she's playing me like a trout on a line. She won't agree to the purchase unless I sign an employment contract, and the minute the sale is final she'll start with the personal stuff. 'Let's talk about that over dinner, Zeke.' 'There's a client's party we must be seen at, so let's go together.' Things like that."

Dana said dryly, "Has anyone ever told you that your ego is the size of South America?"

"You, except I think last time you said Australia."

''Trust me—in the last six years, it's grown. I hate to burst your bubble, Zeke, but if she hasn't actually made her wishes clear, maybe you're imagining things and she really does just want you to work for her.''

''There have been plenty of hints already. A man has instincts about this sort of thing, Dana.''

''Especially a man who doesn't want to be married at all.''

''Honestly, darling, after the first time around, you can't blame me. Maybe you're willing to get burned again, but I'm not.''

''And you actually believe that turning up with a wife will squash her plans? I'd think it's more likely to squash the whole deal instead.''

Zeke shook his head. ''She really does want to buy my business.''

''But what about the employment contract? If you go to work for her, you'll be in almost the same boat in three months as you are now. As soon as she finds out there's a divorce in the works—''

''I have no intention of working for her, and as soon as she realizes that I'm not going to be her tame lapdog, she'll drop her insistence about hiring me. I'd be a rotten employee and she knows it—she'd only put up with me if there were other benefits to having me around. Once she's forced to be realistic about that, we can get down to the serious business of negotiating the last few details.''

''So after the dust settles and the checks are cashed, you can walk away free—from the business, from the CEO, and from the marriage.''

''That's about the size of it.''

To a small degree, Dana couldn't help sympathizing. If the woman Zeke was describing was anything like Barclay, she simply wouldn't take *No* for an answer. Working for someone like that would be next door to impossible...

And that pretty much summed up her own problem, too. How was she going to continue working with Barclay? *I'll have to figure that out later.* ''You're crazy to think a little thing like being married will stop her, Zeke. Women like that specialize in breaking up marriages.''

''It may take a while for her to get the message. That's why I said three months. But as soon as she realizes how madly in love I am—''

"Oh, please. You couldn't carry off that role for fifteen seconds."

His gaze roamed slowly over Dana, caressing every inch of her, and for the first time since she'd come face-to-face with him in the drawing room at Baron's Hill, she felt uneasy. At various times during the evening she'd been angry, puzzled, irritated, confused...but she hadn't truly been uncomfortable. Now, however...

He wasn't touching her—wasn't even sitting close to her—and yet Dana could actually feel his fingertips brushing her face and his breath stirring her hair. She could remember to the last detail how his lips felt against the nape of her neck, the sensitive spot behind her ear, her breast... Her mouth went dry at the memories.

That is enough, she told herself sternly.

But though the errant path of her thoughts had shaken her, it had also steadied Dana's resolve. She'd have to be a fool to get involved with him again, even if it was only in a parody of a marriage. They'd been finished six years ago—nothing changed that. Certainly not some legal loose ends.

But before she could tell him her decision, Zeke said briskly, "See? I can, too, carry it off—that must have been a full minute. Of course, there are some details to take care of, if we're going to be convincing. Shopping, for one. What was Barclay thinking of to let you wear that suit to greet his guests?''

The gibe annoyed her more than it should have, but Dana suspected that was because she agreed with him. If Barclay had given her any warning that he expected her to be the hostess at his party tonight instead of the behind-the-scenes manager, she wouldn't have been wearing a business suit crumpled by a full day of moving furniture, pushing carts, and setting up food tables. She could hardly explain that to Zeke, but ignoring the comment took all of her self-control.

Instead she toyed with a bread stick and asked, ''How are you going to explain to your glamorous CEO why we haven't been living together?''

''Your devotion to your career,'' Zeke said promptly. ''I got tired of a long-distance marriage, and that's why I decided to sell my business in the first place—so I can be with you.''

''Do you have an answer for everything?''

''I try. What about it, darling?''

Dana managed an unsteady laugh. "Look, Zeke, it's been fun watching you tie yourself into knots trying to convince me. But I'm not going to get involved."

He didn't even blink. Instead he reached for his wallet and said, "Give me a minute to settle the bill and I'll take you home."

It was stupid, Dana told herself as she stood near the cash register, waiting for the bartender to make change, to feel disappointed that Zeke hadn't argued or tried to convince her.

Absolutely and utterly stupid.

It had started to rain in earnest, and the Jaguar's wipers beat rhythmically as Dana directed him to her little house not far from downtown. He seemed to have gone very quiet, she thought. Or perhaps it only seemed that way because she didn't feel inclined to chatter.

"I'd be doing you a favor," Zeke said finally.

"How's that?"

"You don't really want to marry Barclay."

Dana's breath caught in her throat. How could he know…? But he couldn't, of course. He was fishing. "Certain of that, are you?"

"Come on, Dana. Do you seriously want your kids to be saddled with the name Howell?"

"What's so bad about it?"

"The nicknames will be killers." The car stopped for a traffic signal, and Zeke looked up at the nearest streetlight and imitated a wolf baying at the moon.

"Howl," Dana said. "Cute. I'll keep that in mind."

"There would be other advantages in co-operating with me."

"Name two."

"Only two? There are dozens. There's always money, though I suppose you'd think it was sordid if I offered to pay you off."

"Depends on how much it was," Dana said thoughtfully. "A few hundred would be sordid. A few hundred thousand, on the other hand, adds an awfully lot of class to a deal."

"I'm thinking of a large enough amount to make a nice dowry."

"*Dowry?* In this day and age? Come on, Zeke."

"I'd suggest tying it up tight in your name, though, because it'll come in handy when you decide to dump Barclay."

"Who says I'm going to dump him? When I get married again it'll be forever— I've made one mistake, and that's enough for a lifetime."

"Trust me, honey. Barclay's certainly an entirely different kind of mistake than I was, but he's still a mistake."

He was dead right about that, even if it was the last thing she'd admit to him. "You were telling me about the advantages of cooperating," she reminded.

"How about the penalties of not cooperating? If I'd fight you, this could drag out for a year or more. Give me a hand, and it'll be over in three months—maybe less—and I'll pay for the divorce. You do realize it isn't going to be cheap this time."

"It wasn't exactly cheap last time, considering that we didn't get what we paid for."

"But if you go ahead now, I'm not paying a red cent. If you're the one who wants the divorce, it's only fair that you be the one to pay for it."

She pointed out a driveway, and the Jaguar pulled in.

Her little cottage was entirely dark, because she hadn't expected to be so late getting home, and it looked deserted and lonely. Also a bit shabbier than usual, Dana thought. The rain had beaten down the overgrown hostas beside the front steps and formed puddles in the low spots in the lawn.

If he didn't like my suit, Dana thought, *he'll no doubt be even more colorful on the subject of the house.*

Zeke tapped his fingers on the steering wheel. ''You should ask the landlord to fix that sag in the gutter.'' He pointed at the corner of the house, where water dripped steadily from a low spot.

''I'm the landlord,'' she said. ''I bought the house just a couple of months ago.''

''In that case, you should move anything you have stored in that corner of the basement, because you'll have water coming in before long.'' He surveyed the open front porch, the cracked paint on the pillars, the loose piece of siding by the front door. ''Did you buy it before you knew Barclay was serious? Or was it a ploy to get him to propose?''

Dana gritted her teeth. ''It had nothing to do with Barclay. I was just tired of paying rent and putting up with upstairs neighbors who had their friends in to dance all night.''

"Well, just remember if you insist on divorcing me, I could ask for half of the house in the property settlement."

"That's fine with me, as long as you take half the mortgage, too." She dug in the side pocket of her handbag for her key.

Zeke put a hand on her arm.

She turned back to face him. It was the first time all evening that he'd touched her, and she was surprised at the urgency of the gesture, startled by how the warmth of his hand seemed to turn the raindrops on her sleeve into steam.

"Think about it, Dana. I'm asking for three months, that's all. Probably not even that much. Get me out of this problem—"

"Get yourself out of it," she said, but her voice was slightly unsteady. "Why don't you confide in your CEO that you're finally getting 'round to divorcing me because you've met the woman of your dreams? A brand-new love affair would be more of a challenge to her."

"I thought of that, but it wouldn't work. If I've been looking around, I could be convinced to look a little harder. Besides, where am I supposed to find someone who'll play the part?"

"Without expecting something lasting to come out of it? Yes, I see what you mean. Poor darling, you do have yourself in a fix."

"That's why you're ideal—she can't possibly compete with a relationship that's been going on as long as ours. We've been married so long you're like a pre-existing condition."

"Gee, thanks," Dana said dryly. "I love being made to sound like a disease. Of course, we've also been separated so long I can hardly remember being married." *Liar,* her conscience whispered. "Which is probably just as well."

Zeke's thumb rubbed gently across the back of her hand, and Dana's nerves shrieked. "It wasn't all bad, you know," he said softly.

No, Dana thought. It hadn't all been bad....

"So what are you going to do?" Zeke asked.

Dana hesitated, but only for an instant. "I'm sure my attorney will be able to find you when it's time to serve the papers." She got out of the car. The wet air outside felt like needles against her face.

"Oh, I'll be around."

"That's what I'm afraid of," she muttered and pushed the car door shut.

He waited in the driveway until she'd unlocked the door and turned on the lights. Then the Jaguar purred down the street and out of sight.

Dana leaned against the front door, eyes closed. Now that it was all over, her head was really beginning to ache.

The first thing she was going to do, she decided, was to dig out her copy of the divorce decree and read every last word. Not that she expected it would do her much good, but at least she'd be familiar with every clause. Then she'd look up the phone number of a good lawyer, so she could call tomorrow for an appointment and take the first step toward ending her marriage. Again.

Though where she was going to scrape up the money was a good question. Even the first consultation wasn't going to be pocket change, because she wasn't about to hire a bargain-basement attorney this time.

If you're the one who wants the divorce, Zeke had said almost casually, *it's only fair that you be the one to pay for it.*

It might be absolutely fair—she couldn't argue with that—but it was also impossible. And whatever he'd said, when it came right down to it, Dana didn't think he'd carry out that threat. He'd said something tonight about the legal bills from the first time around... She frowned, trying to remember. Oh, yes—he'd paid the whole thing, he'd said, because he felt it was his responsibility.

All these years she'd believed that he had walked away from his obligations, leaving her to mop up the financial mess. But he hadn't—he'd taken care not only of his share but of hers. It was completely beside the point that she'd paid the bill, too; it wasn't Zeke's fault that she'd been conned.

But no matter how warm and fuzzy she felt about last time, it didn't make it any easier to find cash now. And serious cash, at that. If she drained her savings account and maxed her credit card...

She hung her raincoat in the tiny front closet beside the front door and crossed the living room to the rolltop desk that had been her father's. She'd been intending to catch up on her bookkeeping tonight anyway. The mortgage payment was due at the end of the week, and the water bill was coming up soon. There wasn't going to be much left of her latest paycheck by the time she was finished.

Maybe Connie knew of an attorney who had a heart—maybe a woman who'd understand and let her make payments on the bill. Or she supposed she could ask Barclay...

The longer Dana thought about it, the better that idea seemed. Barclay must know every high-powered attorney in town. Besides, Zeke had been right about Barclay's tolerance level when it came to a scandal that might affect him personally—it was nonexistent. Asking about an attorney would make the perfect excuse for confiding in him about what a mess she was facing—and once he understood that, he would never say another word about wanting to marry her.

Maybe this whole thing wasn't going to be quite as bad as she'd feared, after all.

Zeke didn't bother to turn on the lights in his hotel room. Not even the red message button on the phone was lit, and thank heaven for that, because it meant that Tiffany hadn't yet figured out where he'd disappeared to. Dana would no doubt snort at the idea that the woman did her utmost to keep track of his every move, but Zeke knew it just the same. It was one of the reasons he had no intention of accepting the too-generous employment package Tiffany had offered.

Tiffany Rowe was the most domineering female he'd ever met, despite the fact that she almost never issued an order. The fact was, however, that the sweet suggestions Tiffany made instead were every bit as definite as if she'd slammed her fist on the table and shouted. The main difference was that if someone disagreed with her, she could act hurt and point out that she'd only been making a suggestion.

An iron core wrapped in feathers and lace— that was Tiffany Rowe in a nutshell. But recognizing what she was didn't make her any easier to deal with. Once the woman had made up her mind it was like splitting the atom to change it.

He lay down on the bed. Now what was he going to do?

Use her own tactics against her, of course. Persistence was the key. If he just kept saying no, politely but firmly, sooner or later she'd get the message.

Yeah, and rain will wash away the Great Wall of China, too. Eventually.

The trouble was, unless he could force Tiffany to believe that he meant what he said, he'd lose the best opportunity he'd ever have to sell his business. Tiffany wasn't the only act in town, but the deal she was offering was the best to be found. If he waited much longer to grab it, the other possible buyers wouldn't be interested anymore—and without competition Tiffany could set her own price instead of paying his.

If he was only looking out for himself, he would thumb his nose at Tiffany and move on to the next prospect. But in the business world, he'd discovered long ago, things were seldom as easy or as straightforward as that.

If Dana would only agree to cooperate... It wasn't like he was asking for the moon. Three months, that was all. Surely there was something she wanted enough to put Barclay off for that long.

As it was, he'd gotten a lot further than he'd expected to tonight. He'd have been contented to get a commitment from Barclay Howell to order the alumni office—notoriously protective of its mailing lists—to cough up Dana's current address. To find her right there at Baron's Hill had been lucky as hell, because it meant he didn't have to go haring off across the country to talk to her.

Of course, his streak of luck hadn't lasted long. It might have been better if he'd had a little longer to think about it. But there was no use wasting time in regrets; he'd made his pitch, and she'd turned him down flat.

Turned him down, for Barclay Howell. The woman was out of her mind.

On the other hand, he thought, he couldn't exactly blame her. The warmth and class and elegance of Baron's Hill must be very tempting to a woman who was living in a rundown little cottage. Dana's house was in one of the better neighborhoods in town, that was true, and it was conveniently close to campus. But she'd obviously bought the runt of the litter. It was going to be a big and expensive job to make the place into the warm, inviting little house it could be.

If she'd bought it only a couple of months ago, reality was probably starting to sink in just about now. So the position and lifestyle that the first lady of the university would enjoy must look very alluring—and Dana was apparently doing all the work of the position anyway. Why settle for a regular paycheck when she could have all the perks as well?

He wondered if she considered Barclay Howell to be a perk of the job, or a drawback.

He reached for the phone and told the night manager at the front desk that he wouldn't be checking out in the morning after all.

He wasn't finished with Dana Mulholland. Not by a long shot.

The morning was bright and sunny, but Dressler Hall always smelled a bit musty for days after a hard rain. Dana wrinkled her nose and made a mental note to open every window in the whole place so that it could air out in time for the start of the academic bowl tomorrow.

She dropped her handbag on her desk and was hanging her coat on the hook on the back of her office door when Connie came in from her office down the hall.

"All right," Connie announced. "You avoided me last night but you can't do it all day. I overhead it all as I was refreshing the hors d'oeuvres table." She pushed Dana's handbag aside so she could perch on the corner of the desk. "So tell me everything that happened."

"If you overheard it all," Dana asked mildly, "why do you need an explanation?"

Connie rolled her eyes. "I mean, I heard all the pieces. At least, I think I heard all the pieces, but putting it together is like doing the jigsaw puzzle without the picture on the box. Who is Zeke Ferris, why does he think you're married to him, and what are you going to do about it? And where does President Howell come into this?"

Take the easy questions first. "President Howell doesn't come into it at all," Dana said. She tried to remember the simple explanation she'd worked out last night. Only, in the light of day, it wasn't very simple and it didn't really explain anything. In fact, it didn't make much sense at all. *I must have been half asleep to think Connie would buy anything of the sort.*

The intercom on her telephone buzzed, and—relieved to have a moment's respite from Connie's questions—Dana answered it. The receptionist in the main office downstairs said, "President Howell is on his way up to see you, Dana." She sounded as if she hardly believed what she was saying.

Dana took her finger off the button, and Connie's eyebrows lifted. ''He doesn't have anything to do with this, huh? You do realize this is the first time in living memory that he's set foot in Dressler Hall rather than summoning us into his presence?''

Barclay had come across campus to see her? The pit of Dana's stomach ached. That must mean that once he'd had a chance to think the whole thing over, he'd realized that Zeke hadn't just been making a bad joke, and he'd decided to cut his losses. If she was lucky, he was just going to break the news that he was withdrawing his offer of marriage. If that was the case, all she had to do was survive a short and uncomfortable conversation, and at least that nightmare would be over.

On the other hand, if she was unlucky...

No, she told herself. Even the president of the university couldn't fire her without going through channels. And he couldn't do it just because she'd embarrassed him, either.

But she wished she had a little longer to think about it. She could already hear the creak of the stairway as he climbed the two flights to her office.

Connie slid off the desk. "Mind if I leave the door open just a crack?" she murmured and went out. A moment later the door opened again and Barclay appeared.

One glance at him and Dana's heart sank. She'd seen him look stern before, but never quite like this.

"Good morning, Dana." His voice was deeper than she'd ever heard it before. "I thought we should talk about how to handle what happened last night. There are bound to be stories going around, of course. It is certainly unfortunate that you hadn't seen fit to tell me about your youthful mistake. There's nothing about it in your personnel file, either."

You read my personnel file before deciding to propose to me? Dana was speechless.

"But it happens," Barclay went on. "People do get divorced. It's just a shame that Zeke Ferris has such an unfortunate sense of humor."

"He wasn't making a joke, sir."

"I think that the best—" Barclay stopped in the middle of a word. "What did you say?"

"I believe he was telling the truth. There was some kind of error in the proceedings, and the divorce never became final."

Barclay's mouth was hanging open.

Dana hurried on. "I'm glad to see you this morning, because I wanted to ask your advice. I'm afraid that unraveling this is going to be a bit difficult, and I'm going to need a good—"

Barclay swallowed hard. "This is indeed a shock."

He sounded like it. His voice had gone thin and squeaky. Dana wondered if his usual deep, resonant boom was a carefully practiced tool and this was the way he really sounded. But she couldn't help feeling just a little sympathetic. It was a big blow to absorb, after all.

"I quite understand, sir," she began. "And of course I don't expect that you—"

Barclay had gone straight on. "I had no idea," he said. "It's only now that I realize... I thought I would have been put off by this, because it's rather squalid, you know. But I'm not. I'm actually not. Dana, I think I might be in love with you."

Dana wanted to groan. Of all the times for Barclay to wax romantic...

"You seemed to be such a practical choice that it never occurred to me that my feelings might include more than simple respect for you. But now I find that I'm willing to wait for you until this difficulty is sorted out." He was obviously feeling both stunned and pleased with himself. "Yes—I'm quite certain. That's what we'll do, then. My popularity with the board of directors will carry us through this little glitch, I'm sure."

And I thought Zeke had an ego. Dana was too stupefied to move, or she'd have seen what was coming in time to put the desk between them. Instead, before she could dodge away, Barclay got an arm around her and pulled her close.

He kissed her as if he'd memorized instructions from a book, first straightforwardly with his mouth closed for a count of five, then slanting across hers for precisely the same length of time. When she felt the tip of his tongue probe against her lips, Dana jerked away.

Barclay gave a breathless little laugh. "Of course you're right, my dear. We shouldn't let ourselves get carried away here, where anyone might walk in. I should have exercised more restraint. It is my responsibility to maintain control."

The great lover, Dana thought. *As if I was so aroused I might pull him down on the cold tile floor...* "We shouldn't let ourselves get carried away at all,'' she said, and fumbled for something—anything!—that would stop him in his tracks. ''Because Zeke and I...well, we've realized that after all these years there's still a certain something between us—''

Distrust. Misgiving. A dash of blackmail.

Barclay goggled at her.

A movement in the doorway caught Dana's eye, and suspicion flooded her as she turned to get a better look.

Zeke's hand was still on the door, pushing it open.

How much had he heard? Dana wondered frantically. And what had he seen?

''Darling,'' he said. ''I know I shouldn't distract you at work, but you forgot to give me a key this morning.'' He strolled across to the desk, dug a hand into the side pocket of her handbag, and pulled out her key ring.

Dana had to give him credit—he'd obviously been paying attention last night because he'd known right where the key ring would be. The effect on Barclay was just about the same as if he'd pulled out a live white rabbit.

''I'll be at home, waiting for you.'' Zeke's voice had dropped almost to a whisper, but Dana knew it was carefully pitched so Barclay couldn't miss a single word. "But in the mean-time, just to refresh your memory about last night..."

He kissed her almost lazily, with the easy certainty of a long-time lover, and only when Dana was completely breathless did he release her and, with a vague half salute to Barclay, leave the room.

He was out of sight before Dana realized that he'd taken her keys with him.

CHAPTER FOUR

AFTER Zeke left, the silence inside Dana's office was deafening. She was too stupefied by Zeke's technique to speak, and Barclay was apparently too thunderstruck. She listened to the thud of Zeke's feet on the wooden stairs—he was obviously wasting no time getting out of range—and tried to remember how to breathe.

It was probably less than a minute, though it felt to Dana like much longer, before Barclay spoke. *"A certain something?"*

"I'm awfully sorry about that," Dana said carefully. "I was trying to warn you..." How could she phrase it, she wondered, so she would leave the impression that she and Zeke had decided to resume their marriage without actually saying it? Nothing less would convince Barclay, but she didn't want to come straight out and lie to him. *We've decided to try it again...we've decided to stay married.* Such a definite announcement was bound to blow up in her face sooner or later. But if she could just imply that they'd reached an agreement without actually uttering the words...

And how are you going to explain that you never see him?

She'd have to cross that bridge when she came to it, Dana decided. It would be a while, at least, before anyone started asking questions. Besides, if she could convince Barclay right now that his courtship was hopeless, he wouldn't even notice what Dana was doing. He'd be too busy reading personnel files again, looking for the next-best candidate to be his first lady. And it was no one else's business how she conducted her supposed marriage.

"I can't blame him for not wanting to let you go," Barclay said finally.

She released a long breath of relief. *Home free. Barclay might be overbearing at times but at least he's honorable.* "It's very sweet of you to understand."

"I know how he feels, my dear, because I feel much the same way. Having just realized that I...that I love you, Dana, I can't possibly give you up."

Dana stared at him. What was it going to take to get through to the man? Maybe the roof of Dressler Hall would conveniently choose this instant to fall in, as it had been threatening to do for years.

She glanced up hopefully, but the roof stayed stubbornly in place. She was on her own, here. "Look, Barclay, the way you're carrying on about this isn't going to win you any points."

"But the difference between us is that Ferris has had his chance," Barclay went on firmly. "While I—"

Inspiration struck, and Dana spoke before she stopped to think. "If you get into a competition with Zeke over me," she warned, "he'll never give the university a dime."

Of course, he isn't planning to anyway, but Barclay doesn't need to know that just now.

Though she'd hoped the suggestion would make him rethink his determination, Dana was startled at how quickly the healthy-looking tan drained out of Barclay's face. "Oh," he said, and the baritone had once more given way to a higher, squeakier voice. "You think that he would...but if I.... I see. You're going back to him in order to persuade him to give generously to the university."

Me and my bright ideas. "I can't guarantee anything," she said hastily.

"That business of his is worth hundreds of millions. If he gives away even ten percent of the proceeds…"

Dana could almost see a calculator clicking in his brain.

Barclay drew himself up straight. "Dana, this is extraordinarily self-sacrificing of you."

He actually believed that she would enter into a bargain like that in order to snag a million-dollar donation for the university, Dana thought in astonishment. But then, she reminded herself, he'd proposed to her in the first place for the sake of the university, because she'd make a good hostess and be a credit to him. So of course he wouldn't see anything odd about a marriage based on money.

"You'll have to leave it entirely to me," she warned. "If you say anything to Zeke about it, you could upset the entire thing."

"Oh, of course. Not a word. I'll leave it entirely in your hands." Barclay rubbed his palms together gleefully as if he was already planning how to spend Zeke's largesse.

"That goes for the board of directors, too," Dana added. "It'll be no good if they start pressing him, or hinting about how badly we need a new stadium.''

Barclay nodded abstractedly. He was still nodding when he left the room. He hadn't even said goodbye.

''So much for him actually being in love with me,'' Dana muttered. ''I have really got to do something about my taste in men.''

At least she'd solved one problem, she congratulated herself. Barclay would leave her strictly alone for the foreseeable future—he wouldn't dare to question her tactics for fear of losing the riches he dreamed of. It would probably be months before he realized that the donation she'd dangled over his head wasn't going to materialize, and in the meantime she could figure out what to do next.

So now she was left with just Zeke.

Just Zeke. As if he wasn't a world of trouble all by himself. For one thing, exactly how much had he heard before he walked into the office a few minutes ago?

Nothing that mattered, she decided, because she hadn't said anything definite. Still, he was bound to wonder why she'd suddenly been trying to put Barclay off.

She threw herself into her chair and stared at the ceiling in despair. How was she going to explain that aberration to Zeke?

And suddenly her answer appeared, as clearly as if it had been written in the stained, patched plaster directly over her head.

It was perfect. It was the solution to all her problems.

Zeke wanted her to postpone filing for divorce for three months. Fine, Dana told herself. She'd do it.

For a price.

Wherever Zeke had gone when he left her office, Dana soon realized that he was deliberately staying out of touch. Not that he would find it especially difficult to avoid her, because she had no idea where he'd spent the night or whether he had any reason to be in town except to find her—but for all practical purposes the man seemed to have fallen off the edge of the world.

"It figures," she muttered. "When I don't want to talk to him, he won't leave me alone. But now that I have something to say..."

It was senseless even to look for him. Still, she tried every hotel she could think of, only to be told that he wasn't registered at any of them. At midafternoon, in desperation, she found herself dialing her home number and listening to the phone ring—as if he'd be crazy enough to pick it up, even if he was there. She slammed the telephone down and told Connie that she was taking the rest of the afternoon off.

"I don't blame you," Connie said. "If that hunk was waiting for me—" She obviously saw the expression on Dana's face, because she swallowed the rest of the sentence. "See you tomorrow, Dana."

The air was crisp and the sun was shining, but the fallen leaves were still soggy underfoot from yesterday's rain. The closer she got to home, the faster Dana found herself walking. Surely Zeke wouldn't be there. But if he had actually had the nerve to go into her house—

Since he'd taken her keys, she'd either have to restrain herself until he opened the door for her or she'd have to stop next door to pick up the spare. And since she was afraid that restraint would be more than she could manage, she'd better hope that Lou or her husband would be at home. They worked the same sort of crazy hours that Dana sometimes did, and they could be hard to catch.

She rounded the last corner, where she could see her house just two doors down, and stopped dead.

Zeke's Jaguar was parked in her driveway, its highly-polished silvery surface glinting in the sun. Standing almost next to it was Lou from next door, holding two coffee mugs.

Zeke himself was perched atop a stepladder at the corner of the house. He was wearing jeans and boots and a pine-green sweater, and a red-gold leaf had caught in his hair. As Dana watched, he gave the once-droopy gutter a twist and with three blows hammered in a spike to hold it tight.

And she'd been afraid that he'd just take over the place. How foolish of her... *Get a grip, Mulholland. Sarcasm isn't going to help the situation.*

"What a lovely surprise it is to find out that Dana's married," the neighbor was saying. "She's seemed so lonely ever since she moved in. I think it's just wonderful that she's not alone anymore. We've never seen her with a man, you know. Of course then we didn't know she was married—*now* I understand why she didn't seem interested.''

That's enough of that, Dana thought, and hurried up the walk. ''Hello, Lou.''

The neighbor grinned at Dana. ''Been keeping secrets, haven't you? You see I've already met your new husband.''

''Not new exactly,'' Zeke said modestly.

''Not new at all,'' Dana put in. ''In fact, if you look closely you'll see that he's pretty frayed around the edges.'' *And he might be feeling even more so by the time I get done with him.*

''That's only because I've been waiting all day to see you again, darling.'' Zeke climbed down from the ladder, pulled off his gloves, and reached for one of the mugs Lou was holding. ''It's awfully nice of you to bring me coffee.''

''My pleasure,'' the neighbor said. ''Dana's a lovely girl, and we're so happy to have her living here. You wouldn't believe the last couple who owned this house—if they weren't yelling at each other, they were sharing sloppy kisses right out in public. Such a relief it was for the neighborhood when they moved out.''

Zeke nodded sympathetically. ''I can imagine.''

''But here I stand yakking when I'm sure you two want your privacy. We'll see you around, I'm sure.''

''I'll bring your coffee cup back later,'' Zeke called after her.

Lou waved and vanished through the gate into her backyard.

Dana waited till she was certain the woman was out of earshot. ''What do you think you're doing?''

''If you want to know why I didn't kiss you hello the moment you arrived, I was just being sensitive to Lou's feelings. You heard what she said about your predecessors. We wouldn't want to embarrass the neighbors with public displays of affection.''

''You mean you didn't want to take the chance that I'd sock you in the jaw.''

''Funny, I didn't feel in any danger when I kissed you this morning.''

''That was because you took me off guard.''

''Oh. I thought perhaps it was because you enjoyed it.''

Enjoyed it? Now that Dana stopped to think about it, however, she realized that there had been something a bit odd about this morning. It was strange that Barclay's kisses had felt entirely clinical despite the passion he said he felt for her, while Zeke's kisses—which had obviously been purely practical—had sizzled clear to her fingertips.

There's nothing personal about it. That's just the difference between an amateur and a pro. "I was asking about *that*." She pointed up at the roof.

"The gutter? I figured this time around we should try the 'what's yours is mine' philosophy instead of this modern marriage business of each taking care of our individual responsibilities. So here I am, fixing our leaky gutter."

"It's not *our* gutter. And you might end up wishing you hadn't tried so hard to impress the neighbors."

"Oh, yes, the neighbors." Zeke's gaze roved over Dana. "So they haven't seen any men around here. Does Barclay not come here at all, or does he only sneak in after dark?"

"I see him every day at the university," Dana said calmly.

"Right. So how did he take the news?"

"Which news would that be?"

"Well, when I popped in this morning you were telling him that we still shared a certain something, so I assumed you were going to announce..."

"Oh, we do share something, Zeke. Suspicion and reservations are the things which immediately come to mind. But despite that, now that I've had a chance to think it over, I'm willing to make a deal."

"Good," Zeke said cheerfully. "Let me take the ladder down and I'll get my—"

"You might want to hear my terms first."

Zeke looked a little wary. "Terms?"

Dana nodded. "You want three months of my life."

"That's the maximum," he pointed out. "If we're lucky—"

"But it might take the whole three months, right? That's as long as we were married the first time around. Pretending for that period of time would be quite a job."

"So what do you want, Dana?"

"Let's sit down and talk about it." She strolled across the lawn to the front steps and perched on the top one. "Not very comfortable, I'm afraid, but better than standing in the driveway. I looked at a porch swing when I first moved into the house. A nice one—teak with striped cushions in jade green and pumpkin.''

''You're asking me for a porch swing?''

''Oh, no, you don't get off that easily. I was just commenting that if I'd realized how nice the weather would stay this fall, I'd have bought it.''

He settled onto the step beside her and balanced his coffee mug on the uneven porch rail. ''I can just see you asking Barclay to hang it. I don't exactly blame him for not coming around. Your list of projects has to be a mile long.''

''I suppose that means you've already been on an inspection tour of the whole house.''

''As a matter of fact, I haven't been inside. I didn't think you'd like it if I used your keys.''

Dana was startled. ''What on earth made you draw the line there?''

''Intuition and sensitivity to your feelings.'' He sounded perfectly serious. ''Also,'' he went on easily, ''I just hadn't gotten around to it. I thought I might as well start with the gutter, so I borrowed the ladder from Lou. I had a pair of gloves in the trunk of the car, and I bought a tool kit at the hardware store because I figured you didn't own a hammer. So I didn't need to go inside.''

Much as she'd like to put him in his place, she had to admit that he was right—she didn't own a hammer. ''Thank you for fixing the gutter.''

''You're welcome.'' He picked up his coffee mug. ''So tell me what you want in return for three months of your life.''

Dana drew her knees up and folded her arms around them. She looked across the street instead of at him, and said, ''A conference center.''

Zeke spit his coffee all the way to the sidewalk. ''You want *what?* You have to be talking a couple of million dollars. Five, maybe.''

''Actually, a nice round ten would be better.''

''Dana, darling, I know I said something last night about a payoff, but you are talking serious money.''

''I know,'' Dana said serenely. ''You can afford it—or at least you will be able to. Barclay told me your business is worth hundreds of millions.''

"Barclay has dollar signs in his eyes. And the sales price isn't all profit, you know. I have obligations—"

"Oh, I understand you'll have to pay off your credit cards first thing. Otherwise the resorts won't even let you onto their beaches. Still, there should be plenty left over to pay for one little...well, all right, medium-size... conference center."

"Credit cards," he said, his tone grumpy. "As if that's the only thing I— You have a pretty high estimation of your worth."

Dana shrugged. "How badly do you want me to cooperate?"

"A conference center." Zeke sounded as if he didn't believe what he was saying.

"The university would probably agree to name it after you."

"What an honor. Why do you want a conference center?"

"Because the university needs it."

"Right. If you were asking for a million for yourself, it would make sense. But ten million for a conference center... Oh, I get it. You *are* going to benefit from this personally."

"I never said I'm entirely altruistic," Dana admitted.

"If you put Barclay on hold for three months while you pretend to be married to me, he's not going to be happy. But if at the end of that time you come back to him with a new conference center in your pocket, he'll forgive you anything. Dana, my dear—"

"Don't call me that."

"What's so bad about it? Oh, I know— that's what Barclay calls you. I'll try to remember that it offends you. I don't think I can manage ten."

"Just add it to the purchase price."

"Oh, that would really go over well with Tiffany."

"Tiffany? Your female CEO's name is Tiffany? How can you possibly take seriously someone who's named after a jewelry store?"

"Wait till you meet her." He sighed. "I could probably find five."

"Skinflint. It's a charitable contribution— you can take every cent of it off your income tax." Dana considered. "Five million outright, and an extra two and a half in matching funds."

"You're a pirate, Dana. I should have you negotiate this sale. All right—if within the next three months Tiffany caves in, gives up the idea of me working for her, and pays the price we've been discussing, you can have your seven-and-a-half mil.'' He dumped the dregs of his coffee on the hostas. ''I'll take the ladder back to Lou. Shall I use the front door or the back to bring in my luggage?''

''You have your luggage with you?''

''I checked out of the hotel this morning.''

''Of course—you were headed back to...wherever it is you live.''

''Minneapolis. No, actually I was planning to move in here.''

''After you sell this business,'' Dana said sweetly, ''you can start up a new one by bottling your extra self-confidence. You'd have an endless supply. Oh, I forgot—no more businesses, only the beach. Which hotel were you staying at? I tried to find you earlier today but none of them seemed to know who I was talking about.''

''That's probably because I didn't use my real name when I checked in. I meant to tell you that last night, but it slipped my mind. Though I guess it doesn't matter now because your attorney won't be trying to find me to serve papers anyway.''

Dana was speechless.

"Back in a minute. As long as I'm going out to the car, would you like me to move it? I assume you have a vehicle in the garage—where would you like me to park the Jaguar so I don't block you in?"

Anywhere on the far side of the Mississippi River, Dana wanted to say. *No, on second thought*—in *the Mississippi would be even better. With you still inside it.* "It's just fine where it is, because I walk to work almost every day. The location was one of the main reasons I bought this house. The other one...you might want to come in before you get your luggage." She stood up. "Oh, and I'd like my keys back, please."

He handed them over without comment.

Dana opened the front door with a flourish. "The other reason I chose this house is because it's small and easy to keep up."

In fact, the cottage was tiny, barely large enough to hold the few bits of furniture that Dana had collected while she lived in student quarters or furnished apartments. The living room held an overstuffed couch, a small table with two wooden chairs, and the rolltop desk and matching swivel chair that she'd inherited from her father. That was all—but there wasn't any space left for more.

Dana stood in the middle of the living room and pointed out doorways. "Coat closet," she said succinctly. "Kitchen. Bathroom. Bedroom—and please note that it's singular. That's all there is."

"What about that one?" Zeke pointed out a narrow door she'd missed, next to the kitchen entrance.

"Unfinished attic. No heat, no windows, no floor, and anybody who's more than five feet tall can't stand up straight except in the exact middle." Not that the living room felt much larger at the moment. How, Dana wondered, did he manage to take up all the available space? She felt as if she could hardly take a breath. "Your options are to sleep on the couch or go back to your hotel. Or to Minneapolis, if you'd rather."

Zeke was looking around as if he didn't believe his eyes. "It wouldn't be a very convincing marriage if we're not living under the same roof."

Dana shrugged. "As far as that goes, if you got a phone call I could always say you were in the shower, and then you could call back from wherever you happened to be.''

''What about unexpected guests?''

''Who's going to drop by here to look for you?''

''I suppose you think Lou won't notice whether I'm living here.''

''As a matter of fact, I don't particularly care what Lou notices. If you hadn't insisted on bringing yourself to her attention—''

''But if she realizes I'm not staying here, she's apt to think it's odd, so she'll probably mention it to the woman down the street who works for the college, and that woman is likely to tell her girlfriend, who'll let it slip to her husband who happens to work for Tiffany's accountant.''

Dana's head was swimming. ''I don't have any idea who you're talking about.''

''The exact individuals are hypothetical— but it's inevitable that there's a network like that. You've obviously underestimated what a small world it is, Dana. How do you think Barclay found me yesterday, anyway?''

''I hadn't given it a thought.'' But now that he mentioned it—if he hadn't been using his real name at the hotel…how *had* Barclay issued that invitation?

"A former professor of mine was having breakfast in the hotel dining room. He recognized me, and before I could stop him he'd whipped out his cell phone and called Barclay to tell him that a distinguished alumnus was in town."

"I doubt that Lou will be calling up Tiffany for lunch anytime soon," Dana said dryly. "But it's up to you."

"Seven and a half million," he muttered, "and she offers me the couch."

"Take it or leave it. Because even seven and a half million doesn't buy you a ticket into my bedroom, Zeke."

"I'll take it." Zeke started for the front door. "By the way, don't even think about trying to lock me out. While I was at the hardware store, I had them make a duplicate set of your keys." The door banged behind him.

"He says he's too polite to come in without my permission," Dana muttered. "But he makes himself a set of keys… Ha!" She went into her bedroom and, from the top of her small closet, dug out a pillow, a set of sheets, and a couple of blankets. She piled them prominently on the end of the couch and went on to the kitchen to make a pot of coffee.

She heard a thump as a suitcase hit the oak floor in the living room, and a minute later Zeke appeared in the kitchen.

"Don't ask what's for dinner," Dana said, "or I will pour boiling coffee over your head."

"Do you still like Polynesian?" He reached for the telephone book.

"I never liked Polynesian. I only said I liked it because I was foolish enough to want to please you."

Zeke looked up intently. "That's odd, because I never liked it all that well myself. I thought you did. In that case, we'll have Chinese."

"I'm tired of Chinese. At least we've settled one thing." Dana reached for a mug. "We aren't going to waste time and effort bending over backward to be polite to each other."

"I don't recall that we did before, either. If we had, perhaps we'd still be married for real. Mind if I have a cup of coffee?"

"You just had one."

"Yours smells better."

"Careful or I'll tell Lou." She handed him an empty mug.

He paused in the act of pouring his coffee to stare at the kitchen sink, where the faucet dripped steadily at the rate of once a second. ''No wonder you asked if I'd already inspected the place. If I had, I might not have brought my suitcase in.''

''I'm not asking you to do anything about it,'' Dana said.

''Oh, I might as well stay busy till I can hit the beach and start working on my tan.''

''How about staying busy by looking after your business? If you ignore it for the next three months, Tiffany might not be willing to pay as much.''

''And it would be such a shame if you didn't get your conference center after all.''

''Maybe I should have put that in writing,'' Dana muttered.

''Besides, unless you're planning to skim off a little of that seven and a half million, you'd better take advantage of cheap labor where you can find it. If you're moving into Baron's Hill anytime soon, you'll be wanting to sell this place, and—frankly—it needs all the help it can get.''

Cheap labor. Well, he might not send her a bill—but Dana had a nasty feeling that she'd be paying an emotional price for the next three months, and it would end up being far from cheap.

CHAPTER FIVE

ZEKE lost the coin toss, so he went to pick up their takeout order from the Greek restaurant on the edge of downtown. He gathered up the boxes of moussaka and *dolmades* and then had to set them down again to reach for his wallet so he could pay the bill.

Figures, he thought. *She sticks me up for seven and a half million and the dinner check, too.*

He had to confess to feeling a twinge of admiration for Dana, however—though he'd sooner let the chef at the Greek restaurant grind him up and stuff him into a bunch of grape leaves than admit it to her. If she'd asked for a few million for herself, he'd have written her off as a gold digger, and though he'd have been a bit disappointed in her, he wouldn't have been surprised.

He could understand why she would think she had a right to some serious cash. She hadn't been joking last night about how they'd lived on rice and beans during the short time they'd been married. And though he wouldn't have admitted it at the time, without her he might not have made it through the crucial last semester of his schooling.

So he probably did owe her a good chunk of his assets—and he was reasonably sure her attorney would agree, whenever they got to that stage.

But to try to nick him for ten million bucks for a conference center, of all things... If the whole deal hadn't smelled a bit like extortion, she'd deserve to be named employee of the year.

Unless she was doing it entirely for Barclay.

"Sir," the waitress called after him. "You forgot your wine."

He juggled the boxes so he could grab the neck of the bottle, and by the time he got the whole mess into the car he was seriously short of patience. Greek restaurants didn't believe in bags, for heaven's sake?

When he got back to Dana's cottage, she'd changed her suit for jeans and a dark blue sweater emblazoned with the university's logo, and she was setting the small table in the living room with chunky pottery plates and bright-colored napkins. She opened the door for him when he kicked the bottom panel and took the boxes out of his arms.

He hung his jacket on the doorknob and watched her cross the room to set the boxes on the table. *That answers one question,* he thought. *She's still got the nicest-shaped little rear on campus.*

"The table for two looks very domestic," he said.

Dana shrugged. "Don't expect candle-light—but I figure for seven and a half million, I can set the table without complaining."

She sat down before he could offer to hold her chair, and while he opened the wine bottle she served the food. She didn't look up at him. "I was thinking while you were gone."

"That sounds dangerous," Zeke observed.

"I suppose I should at least find out a little about your business."

"Might not hurt. What do you want to know?" He picked up a fork.

"For one thing, why Tiffany wants so badly to buy it."

"Because it's a very profitable little produc-tion line that fits right into her business strat-egy. We make switches, she makes the machines that use them, so it's utterly sensible to combine the two.''

Dana frowned. ''What makes the switches so special?''

His explanation had been perfectly straightforward, but he'd almost forgotten that gift of hers for asking questions that seemed pointless but which went straight to the heart of the problem. ''Well, I don't like to sound as if I'm bragging—''

''Oh, go right ahead and brag. I promise not to take you seriously.''

She didn't even sound sarcastic. *Now that she's getting regular practice,* Zeke thought, *she's much better at it.*

He said dryly, ''Good—I'd hate to have you thinking I was some kind of genius. A few years back I came up with an idea for a new way to trigger an electrical switch.''

''How many ways are there?''

''You'd be surprised. Light, sound, vibration, radio waves...anyway, this was something that had never been done before, but it worked.''

''Is it top secret or something?''

''Not exactly. But it would take half the night just to explain the physics of it.''

"That's all right. We've got three months to kill, so we might as well spend one night of it on a physics lesson." She sounded distracted.

He watched her pick at her moussaka. Her head was bent, and her hair, which had been pulled back tightly when she came home from work, was loose around her shoulders. It was wavy from being wrapped in a bun all day, and it gleamed like copper in the light of the sconce above the table. Her hair was darker than he remembered, or was that just a trick of the subdued lighting in the room? And was it still as soft?

We've got three months to kill, she'd said. He could think of better ways to spend the next ninety days than discussing physics. A whole list of better ways, in fact....

She looked up, fork suspended. "Zeke?" She sounded suspicious.

He tugged his mind back to the moment. *You said it yourself, Ferris. Thinking's dangerous—so knock it off.* "I'd hate to bore you to sleep with the details. But in a nutshell that's why Tiffany wants to buy me out—because she wants the patents."

"Why not keep it yourself? You've obviously made a success of it so far."

"Being successful in business is damned hard work, Dana."

"And you'd rather lie on a beach. Well, I suppose you have something there." She teased a bit of eggplant loose. "So tell me why you think Tiffany's going to believe that we're happily-ever-aftering when she's never heard of me before. How have we even—supposedly—been seeing each other?"

"I stop by whenever I visit customers in the area." He let a hint of longing creep into his voice. "But a stolen night—and day, of course—here and there isn't nearly enough to satisfy either one of us. As a matter of fact, I've only been here a few hours and I'm already thinking about how it'll feel to be away from you again."

"Likewise," Dana said dryly. "It's such a shame that you have to go back at all... Come on, Zeke—you honestly think she'll buy that?"

"Obviously you don't. Look, every now and then you hear about a guy who's kept two families for years and even the wives didn't suspect. So why couldn't I have kept one wife secret from somebody I wasn't even dating?"

"Because you'd have been more likely to keep me secret if you *were* dating her."

"If you have a better idea, sweetheart, now's the time."

"Well...I'd suggest something a little closer to the truth. We've had a rocky time of it, which is why you haven't talked about me—the whole thing has been too painful to discuss. But now we've..." Her voice trailed off.

"What is it, Dana?"

"You know, it doesn't make any sense at all that you'd sell a successful business for the sake of my career."

"I'm doing it because you're a stubborn, liberated little feminist and you wouldn't agree to give up your job."

"But you're supposedly putting a multi-million-dollar business on the block because I like running a conference center? There are other jobs like this one. Even some in Minneapolis, I'm sure."

Zeke shrugged. "You're attached to this one, since you've raised the money for the building and all."

"Then why not move your business here?"

"Too complicated. I'd have to disrupt the lives of a couple of hundred employees."

"And selling the company out from under them won't be unsettling enough?"

"It will without a doubt cause some changes in their lives," Zeke said.

"Well, I'd suggest you get your story in line before you launch this fairy tale."

"Too late. I called my office this afternoon to announce that I'd be running things from here for a while—and I explained why."

Dana dropped her fork. It hit the edge of the pottery plate with a clang and bounced onto the floor. She didn't seem to notice.

"So you get your wish," he added. "I don't have to go back at all."

"Damn," she said softly.

"Dana, if you're going to tell me it isn't convenient for you to put Barclay on hold right now, you're a little late."

"No, it's not that. I just realized I should have held out for the whole ten million. You wouldn't have had any choice but to agree."

He grinned at her. "Pirates have to take their chances." He went to the kitchen and brought her another fork. "How close are you to having the funds raised to build the conference center, anyway?"

"With your generous contribution," she said sweetly, "very close."

"Does the job keep you busy?"

"It will when the new building's finished. In the meantime, though, we can only handle smaller events, so that's why I've been taking care of Baron's Hill while the butler's been on sick leave."

"I wondered if you were going to try to keep on handling it all. It wouldn't leave much time for Barclay. Did you come back here because of him, or did you meet him after you got here?"

She hesitated just long enough to make him curious. "I was here before he came. The idea was to create demand for a conference center while we were still raising funds, so it'll be busy just as soon as it's built."

"And I suppose it's easier to convince people to make a donation if they've tried to hold an event in Dressler Hall."

A smile tugged at the corner of her mouth. "That is a factor, yes."

He spooned another *dolmades* onto his plate. "So you weren't away from here very long, were you?"

"A few years. I came back just about eighteen months ago. I was working in Chicago, in a hotel, when I heard about the job. It sounded interesting, so I came up to look." She pushed her plate away.

And obviously, Zeke thought, that was all she was going to say.

She'd played with the moussaka, but she'd eaten hardly anything, he realized. No wonder there were such interesting hollows under her cheekbones and at the base of her throat. Furthermore, he'd bet that on the average day she didn't find time for lunch, either. Not that it was any of his business.

The woman needs a nanny. And you're not it, Ferris.

Dana took care of the leftovers, staying in the kitchen as long as she could, and then used the excuse of the high school academic bowl to retreat to her bedroom. "The students will be there first thing in the morning to start the competition," she said. "But before they can actually begin, I'll have to show all the volunteer question-readers what to do, so I really need to be there an hour before the official start time." She saw Zeke's eyebrows tilt and added wryly, "Yes, I did just say I'll have to teach them how to read. The students can only listen, they can't look at the questions—so there's a definite knack to making everything clear by using only the tone of voice. Haven't you ever watched a game show?"

He looked as if he didn't believe a word of the explanation.

"Make yourself at home," she said sweetly. *As if he hasn't already.* "I think I put out everything you'll need. I do hope you'll be comfortable on the couch."

"No, you don't," she heard him mutter as she closed her bedroom door.

But her room wasn't quite the sanctuary she'd expected it would be. However ill-at-ease Zeke might be on the narrow couch, Dana wasn't much better off. Did that creak come from the house shifting slightly as the outside temperature dropped, or was he still moving around in the living room?

It shouldn't be any surprise if he was, because he'd always been a night owl. That had been part of the problem....

I am not going to lie awake tonight contemplating what went wrong with my marriage, she told herself firmly. Just because there was

a very large and solid reminder out in her living room didn't mean she had to obsess over
past mistakes. She'd learned her lesson, and
there was no reason whatsoever to go back
over old ground.

She had been very young, she reflected, and
pitifully romantic. She had believed that love
would overcome all obstacles, all differences.
And there was no question that she had loved
him. Who wouldn't have? In those days, Zeke
had been charming and funny and lovable and
enticing, everything she thought she wanted in
a life partner.

And a whole lot more, she thought wryly.
He'd also been stubborn and hardheaded and
single-minded—at least on certain subjects.
And he, too, had had a vision of what marriage
should be—a vision that was completely different from Dana's. If they'd had enough sense
to take some time to get to know each other
first, they would probably never have married
in the first place.

And she wouldn't be in this fix now—with
an almost-ex-husband camped out just beyond
her bedroom door.

Another creak. This time she was sure it was
the hardwood floor in the living room. Zeke

hadn't settled down for the night yet—if he ever could, on that lumpy and too short couch.

Not that it was her problem. He could have gone back to the hotel and been comfortable. For that matter, he could have gone all the way back to Minneapolis and made his explanations in person. What did he think Dana was going to do, anyway—pack up and run away if he turned his back?

Not with seven and a half million dollars at stake, that was sure. She could certainly put up with having Zeke in her living room for three months, with that prize dangling within her reach.

Maybe, she thought with a yawn, she could do more than just put up with him....

The thought jolted her awake. What in heaven's name was she thinking about? She didn't want him back. She had learned that lesson the hard way, and she would never put herself through that sort of pain again.

But where she'd made her mistake was in trying to build a life with the man. Now she knew better, and she wouldn't fall into that trap again.

But that didn't mean she couldn't enjoy herself in the meantime. Zeke was obviously still every bit as charming and funny as he'd ever been. If she'd only been wise enough not to marry him—not to expect more than he could give—they might still have been friends.

So why couldn't they be friendly now?

There was a peculiar sort of satisfaction in the idea of zinging him for seven and a half million dollars...and having fun while she did it.

Maybe, she thought as she drifted off, tomorrow morning she'd ask him if he wanted to be buddies.

But Zeke was gone when Dana got up the next morning. He hadn't been gone long, for the coffee he'd left in the pot was still fresh. And he was intending to come back, because he'd left all his belongings. She didn't even realize she'd looked for his things until she felt a wash of relief when she spotted his suitcase tucked under the table.

But why on earth should she feel relieved by the evidence that he intended to stay? She should have been happy to see the back of him.

On the other hand, she reminded herself, she had seven and a half million excellent reasons to want him to stick around.

He had not, of course, left her a note. But then he had no particular obligation to let her know where he was going. In a sense he was a tenant—and a very-high paying one at that—so he didn't have to keep the landlady informed of his movements.

And why would he have felt it necessary to give her an explanation now, Dana asked herself, when he hadn't during their marriage? One of the big points of conflict in their months together had been Zeke's tendency to disappear without warning for hours at a time. Married people didn't do that, she had tried to explain to him, and he'd told her in return that being married didn't mean he couldn't breathe without asking her for permission. It had been a regular cause for disagreement, recurring with greater frequency and at higher volume— right up to and including their final argument. Or perhaps it would be more accurate to say that it had been the beginning of that last fight, because it certainly hadn't ended there.

Let it be a lesson to you, Dana thought. *He's just as stubborn and single-minded and self-centered as ever.*

She turned off the coffeepot and locked the front door behind her. The Jaguar was in the driveway, but there was no evidence of Zeke anywhere around. Wherever he'd gone...

It's none of your concern, Dana told herself firmly.

It was another crisp and lovely fall morning, perfect for walking to work. She was halfway to the campus when she heard the thump of footsteps on the sidewalk behind her, and she automatically moved to one side to let the jogger pass.

Instead, Zeke dropped into step beside her. He was wearing tight-fitting jogging shorts and a sweatshirt with the sleeves pushed up above his elbows, and his hair was standing almost on end. He was breathing a little faster than normal, but there was no other evidence that he'd had a workout. At his heels was a dog. A big dog, she noted, with long floppy ears, an uptilted nose, and feet the size of saucers.

"Good morning." Dana kept walking. "Who's your pal?"

"He appeared out of nowhere when I was a few blocks from the house. He has a collar but no tags, and he didn't seem to have anything better to do than go jogging, so he joined me."

"Well, I suppose it's a change from chasing cars."

''If you've seen him chasing cars, then you must know where he belongs.''

''Don't all dogs chase cars if they have the chance?'' Dana looked down at the animal and shook her head. ''No, I'm sure I'd remember if I'd seen him before. He looks like a mixture of black Labrador and rhinoceros.''

''Hush, you'll hurt his feelings. Don't listen to her, Midnight, she's just being rude.''

''If he doesn't have tags, how do you know his name?''

''It seemed an obvious choice, considering the color of his coat, so I tried it and he responded.''

''Something tells me if you'd called him Whitey he'd have answered, too. Here, Rhino!''

The dog's head popped up, his eyes brightened, his tail wagged, and he pranced toward her.

''I rest my case,'' Dana murmured. ''Do you run every day?''

''No. Only when I can't sleep. That has to be the lumpiest couch in the western hemisphere.''

''Taken a regular poll of them, have you?''

"No," he drawled. "Generally when I'm an overnight guest I don't spend my time on the couch. What's with you this morning? Oh, I suppose you're teed off because I didn't leave you a note."

"Certainly not. It's none of my business where you go. If you're planning to disappear for more than a couple of days, it would be thoughtful of you to let me know, but—"

"So you won't report me to the police as a missing person?"

"No," she said pleasantly. "So I won't call the Salvation Army to come and pick up your clothes. I wouldn't dare call the police, because I wouldn't have any idea what name to give them. Which reminds me, you never explained why on earth you were using a fake name at the hotel."

"Because I didn't want to leave a trail."

"For whom? Tiffany? You don't really think she's following you."

"Following, no. Watching, yes. I thought it would be just as well if nobody—particularly Tiffany—realized that I had to make a stop at our mutual alma mater before I could catch up with you."

"Since you're supposed to have known all along where I was," Dana said.

"Exactly. But I didn't know if I'd find you hanging out in Seattle or Fort Lauderdale or somewhere in between, so it might have been a little difficult to explain a side trip to Wisconsin."

"I see. Personally, I think you have a trench-coat complex and you're seeing shadows where there isn't even any sunlight, but if it makes you happy—"

"Oh, it does," he assured her. "I'm at my best when I'm plotting a conspiracy."

"So what are you going to do today? Besides conspiring, I mean."

"Buy a bed."

"There's nowhere to put one."

"There will be if I drag the couch out to the curb for the garbage collectors."

"Don't you dare. I like my couch, and it had better still be inside the house when I get home tonight." Dana stopped beside the front steps of Dressler Hall. "Got it, pal?"

"Yes, ma'am," Zeke murmured.

She started to turn away, so his kiss landed off target, on her cheekbone instead of her mouth. She pulled back in surprise. "What do you think you're doing?"

"Demonstrating affection—which is going to be a little hard to do if you jump a foot every time I come near you."

"You startled me, Zeke."

"We're going to have to work on that."

"What? Startling me?"

"No. Demonstrating affection."

She eyed him warily. "If you're suggesting that we need practice, forget it."

"It's not going to be very convincing if you obviously can't stand for me to touch you, Dana."

"Oh, I can stand it just as well as you can." She raised one hand to his cheek, then let her fingertips slide over his ear and through his hair to nestle at the back of his neck. She tugged his head down, stood on her toes, and kissed him, letting her eyes drift shut as if she was closing out everything around her and leaving only him.

For about three seconds, she was in charge—just long enough to reassure her that there was nothing so very frightening about kissing him, and nothing so very special about it, either. She could do this as often as necessary to convince Tiffany, she told herself. There was nothing to it. All she'd have to do was think about her seven and a half million dollars, and she would look as though she were lost in a faraway world.

Then Zeke moved, and somehow in an instant Dana lost all control of the situation. Suddenly she wasn't holding on to him because the pose looked good, she was hanging on because the world was swirling around her and she needed his solidity as a brace. He had pulled her close, and his mouth against hers was teasing, tormenting, promising delights.

When he'd kissed her the day before in her office, she'd thought that she'd been paralyzed because he'd taken her by surprise. But this time she had initiated the kiss herself—and she was still helpless in his arms. Not because he was holding her against her will, for Dana knew instinctively that she could break free. The trouble was, she didn't want to.

Eventually he released her mouth, but he didn't stop kissing her. He nibbled his way across her cheekbone, grazed for a moment on her earlobe, and unerringly found the ticklish spot on the side of her neck. Dana's head jerked back.

"See?" Zeke said, sounding entirely unmoved. "That's what I said—we have to work on this tendency of yours to jump whenever I touch you." He whistled for the dog, and a moment later the pair of them were rounding the corner of Dressler Hall, jogging easily.

Dammit, Dana thought. He hadn't even been short of breath.

Dressler Hall was packed tight with more than two hundred high school students, their teachers, the volunteer judges and the question-readers. At the beginning of the day, every room in the building—including Dana's office—held two competing teams and another pair waiting their turn. But as the day wore on and teams were eliminated, the pressure eased a little.

By late afternoon Dana managed to slip away for a short break, and she was searching her desk for an aspirin when Connie tapped on the door and came in. "What now?" Dana asked with foreboding.

"No problems to report, for a change. We're down to the last round of the day, and enough of the teams have already left that I think it's safe to say the building won't split down the corners—at least till tomorrow, when they all come back to watch the finals.''

"That's some relief," Dana said.

"If you want to go home early, I can handle everything here till it all winds down." Connie glanced at the clock behind Dana's desk. "In another hour they'll all be descending on the pizza parlors downtown anyway."

Dana found the aspirin bottle and dumped two tablets into her palm. "And in return...?"

Connie grinned. "You know me pretty well, don't you? Today's our anniversary and my husband's taking me out for dinner tonight. Not pizza, I might add. But I'd like to sleep in tomorrow."

"Sure," Dana said. "I'll be here at the crack of dawn anyway, but it won't take both of us since all the readers and judges know what they're doing now. We have enough volunteers for tomorrow, don't we?"

"I've got a list somewhere."

"That's all right. We don't need nearly as many since we've eliminated half the teams. See you whenever you get up tomorrow, then." Dana scooped up her handbag and headed for the door.

On the stairs, she met Mrs. Janowitz, wearing the dark purple vest that marked her as a volunteer question-reader. Dana had seen her across the hall as they switched rooms earlier, but it was the first time she'd come face-to-face with the woman since the afternoon tea at Baron's Hill when Mrs. Janowitz had whispered her approval. Now she looked anything but approving, Dana thought warily.

Dana said a cheery hello and would have passed straight by, but Mrs. Janowitz stepped into her path. "I must tell you, Dana," she said coldly, "that I am shocked. *Shocked!* The very idea that you would treat Barclay like that—"

Dana bit her tongue to keep from saying that if Barclay had showed enough sense to tell his prospective bride what he had in mind before he shared it with the rest of the campus, he wouldn't have been embarrassed by the outcome.

"And I'm hurt," Mrs. Janowitz went on. "Absolutely wounded that you would lead him on, when you're a married woman. And I'm also stunned that you place so little importance on the reputation of the university as to carry on as you were doing on the front steps of Dressler Hall this morning.''

Of course, Dana thought, Mrs. Janowitz would have been there to see that kiss. It was inevitable. ''I couldn't agree with you more about the incident on the steps,'' she said mildly. ''It was quite wrong of me to forget myself like that, and I assure you I'll do my absolute best to keep it from happening again.''

She slipped past and left Mrs. Janowitz still sputtering on the stairs.

Dana walked home as slowly as she could, hoping that the sunshine and clear air would soothe away her headache before she had to confront Zeke. But as soon as she turned the corner the pain came back as if she'd been hit with a hammer.

Lying on the sidewalk in front of her house was the dog that had been tagging along at Zeke's heels that morning. He was sprawled across the cool concrete, his tongue dangling. And next to him were two big, shiny stainless-steel bowls, one full of water and one containing only crumbs of dog food. He got up and ambled toward the door with her, indicating quite clearly that he'd like to come in.

When Dana pushed the door open, she was already yelling Zeke's name.

"I'm in the kitchen," he called back. "Lou's teaching me to make a pot roast."

Dana stopped in mid-rant. She took a deep breath and walked slowly across the living room, detouring around a large box in the middle of the floor. On the side of the box was a picture of an inflatable mattress which looked large enough to carpet the whole room, and an air pump sat beside the box, ready for use.

She gritted her teeth and followed the scent of onions into the kitchen. "Hello, Lou."

The neighbor grinned from her perch beside the stove, where Zeke was bending over a roasting pan in the oven. "He's going to be a good house-husband, this one," she said.

For about sixty seconds, Dana thought. *Until I choke him with a half-cooked potato.*

"Would you mind telling me," she said gently, "what the dog is doing out front?"

"Guarding," Zeke said. He closed the oven door. "I thought that was obvious."

"Guarding his food bowl, maybe. Why is he still here?"

Lou laughed. "I told you not to feed him, Zeke."

Zeke shrugged. "I called all the radio station lost-and-found numbers, so they can broadcast a description."

"Oh, that should have people lined up wanting to claim him," Dana muttered.

"But there haven't been any calls, and he was obviously hungry, so I fed him."

"You bought him a special food dish?"

"I didn't think you'd like it if I used your mixing bowl."

"You got that much right." The doorbell rang and Dana brightened. "Maybe this is his owner now. Unless the rhino knows how to press doorbell buttons."

Zeke dropped the fork he'd been using to test the roast and followed her.

Dana eyed him suspiciously. "If you're going to require proof of ownership, or try to make sure that he's going to a humane home, forget it, Zeke." She pulled the door open.

The dog surged in, almost knocking her over. Dana recovered her balance and saw a petite blonde in a pastel pink suit standing in the doorway.

Odd sort of owner for a mutt like that, Dana thought. *I'd think she's more the Persian kitten type.*

The blonde's big blue eyes roved over Dana, the dog, the box on the floor, the air pump, the blankets and sheets stacked on the arm of the couch, and Zeke. "Well, hello, Zeke," she said. "Remind me to buy you an apron for a wedding present. It comes a few years late, I'm afraid, but it's obviously the most suitable thing I could get you—strings and all." She held out a hand to Dana. "I'm Tiffany Rowe. And you must be the little wife."

CHAPTER SIX

DANA had always thought that the idea of a drowning person seeing his life flash before his eyes was something of an exaggeration. Now she knew better, because in the split second she stood there looking at Tiffany Rowe's outstretched manicured fingertips, Dana could see not only her past but her future. And she didn't like the looks of it. In fact, she had a nasty feeling that she was watching seven and a half million dollars waving goodbye.

Not if I can help it, she thought. *At least I can go down fighting.*

She shook Tiffany's hand. "Nice to meet you. I'm Dana Mulholland." Her voice was huskier than usual, but she comforted herself that Tiffany had no way of knowing that.

Tiffany's neatly-plucked eyebrows arched. "Mulholland? Not Ferris?"

Dana could have swallowed her tongue. It was hardly a crime these days for a woman not to take her husband's name, but under the circumstances, anything which caused questions could be dangerous. If Tiffany didn't believe this performance…

"Dana's a career woman through and through," Zeke said. "Things like names and jobs and independence are very important to her."

"But rings don't seem to be," Tiffany observed.

Against her will, Dana's gaze shot to her own bare left hand.

Zeke hadn't paused. "That's why I'm giving up my business—so we can be together."

Tiffany smiled at him. Though it would be more accurate, Dana thought, to say that she showed her teeth—because there was no amusement in the expression. "How odd that you've never said anything about that particular reason before, Zeke."

Zeke smiled just as broadly. "Well, of course I didn't confide all my secrets. I want to sell my business, Tiffany, not give it away. Surely you wouldn't expect me to tell you exactly how anxious I was to sell until after you'd made an offer."

"There's nothing signed yet," she reminded him.

Zeke shrugged. "We've pretty much made the bargain. What's left to decide is only details. That's why I concluded there was no point in delaying my move any longer."

"Because your wife needs you now," Tiffany murmured.

Dana decided she'd stayed on the sidelines long enough. "That's right. I need him desperately." She put a possessive hand on Zeke's arm, and he cupped his fingers over it and smiled down at her.

It was a dazzling smile, and even though Dana knew it was only a performance, it still made her feel warm all over.

"But if she's so self-sufficient, what does she need you for?" Tiffany mused. Her big blue eyes summed Dana up and then her gaze drifted around the room, surveying not only the living room but the areas beyond the open doorways.

"I wouldn't think I'd have to explain that to you, Tiffany," Zeke said gently.

Something about the tone of his voice not only drained all the warmth out of Dana but sent chills up her spine. He sounded as if the woman had firsthand, intimate knowledge of what he had to offer...but he'd told Dana that he hadn't even dated Tiffany. He couldn't have slept with her.

Could he?

He's speaking generally, Dana thought. *A woman like that...she's bound to have had affairs. That's all he meant.*

"There's the obvious, of course," Tiffany said. "But on the other hand..." She pointed at the corner of Dana's sleigh-backed bed, just visible through the open doorway, and then gave a sidelong glance at the air mattress, still in its box in the center of the floor. "You seem to have a perfectly adequate bed. Quite large enough for two. And yet here's another one, and it's clearly a new addition to the household."

"Oh, that." Dana desperately looked around for any possible explanation.

"Rather like Zeke, as a matter of fact," Tiffany said calmly. "A *very* new addition to the household. How interesting."

From the corner of her eye, Dana caught a flicker of movement in a shadowed corner of the living room. She'd forgotten that when Tiffany rang the bell, the dog had managed to duck inside. "The air mattress is for the dog," she said firmly.

At the same moment, Zeke began, "Dana hasn't been feeling well, so in order to allow her to rest comfortably—"

Tiffany looked from one to the other and then to the dog. "Well, I've heard of husbands being relegated to the doghouse," she murmured, "but not to the dog's bed. Whose animal is it, anyway?"

"Ours," Zeke said firmly.

"I see. My goodness, you are settling into domestic life, Zeke. A wife *and* a dog."

The dog, as if he knew he was being discussed, wriggled in between Zeke and Dana, gave a long sigh, and leaned his enormous head against Dana's hip, almost knocking her over again.

Zeke steadied her, then grabbed the animal's collar and hauled him toward the door.

"Next he'll be trading the Jaguar in on a minivan," Dana murmured. "And he's really looking forward to being a soccer coach."

Zeke paused as if the idea had hit him like an arrow. Dana tried to smother her grin. The vision of Zeke with a whistle and a midget soccer team was obviously too much for him to take in.

He recovered in a moment and opened the door to push the dog out, just as Connie, who was standing on the porch, raised her hand to knock.

For an instant they were frozen into a tableau, Dana and Tiffany facing off and Zeke pushing the dog, who clearly did not want to leave. The look on Connie's face as she took in the scene was priceless, but as she opened her mouth, dread flooded through Dana. She had no idea what Connie might say.

Dana slid past Zeke and almost pushed Connie across the porch toward the front steps, pulling the door shut behind her with Zeke and the dog still inside. Zeke swore and the dog let out a mournful howl. "Make up your mind, Rhino," Dana muttered and opened the door enough to let the animal out. He gave her a drool-filled grin and sat down on her feet.

Dana eyed Connie. "What are you doing here? I thought you were going out for dinner."

"I was. I mean, I am. But we've got a problem." Connie jerked a thumb over her shoulder, and for the first time Dana looked past her, realizing there was a teenage girl standing behind Connie, half hidden in the shadow of the porch pillar. "Actually, it's more of a simple mixup. Alison's here for the academic bowl, but she can't stay in the dorm with the other kids."

"Why on earth not?"

The teenager stepped forward. "For a completely ridiculous reason," she said. "I have asthma, and my mother's afraid I'll have an episode—so she insists I have adult supervision around the clock. As if I don't take care of my own medications at home."

"Well, I can see her point," Dana mused. "Mothers are funny that way. What about your school sponsor? Your team has a chaperone, right?"

"Male," Connie said briefly.

"And my mother doesn't trust him, anyway," the teenager volunteered. "She thinks he'd panic if I started to wheeze."

"I see. Connie, why didn't we know about this ahead of time?"

"We did," Connie admitted glumly. "Or at least we were supposed to. The letter asking for special treatment came last week, but it got set aside and it vanished under a bunch of other stuff."

The only surprise there, Dana thought, was that it didn't happen more often. She tried not to turn the offices in Dressler Hall into meeting rooms, but sometimes she didn't have any choice—the academic bowl wasn't the only event big enough to require every room she could find. And every time a desk had to be cleared so the room could be used, the odds were that something would be lost or overlooked or neglected. She'd done it herself often enough.

"I found the letter after Alison's chaperone asked at the end of the day where she was supposed to go," Connie said miserably. "I'm really sorry, Dana, but I didn't know what else to do with her. I've nagged my husband for weeks so he wouldn't forget our anniversary. If I cancel this dinner tonight, he'll never speak to me again."

"What about Professor Wells? She's got that nice condo—"

"She's also got cats," Connie reminded. "Half a dozen of them. And Alison's allergic. You're it, Dana."

Dana was starting to lose the feeling in her toes. She tried to shift the dog's weight off her feet, but he settled in more firmly. She looked at the girl. "What about dogs? Are you sensitive to them, too?"

"I've never noticed a problem," the teenager said cautiously. She put out a hand to pat the dog, and he leered at her. His tail swished across Dana's knees, tickling madly.

"Meet the rhino," Dana said with resignation. "I have to warn you that this isn't exactly a four-star resort, but you're very welcome. Do you have a bag?"

Alison went off to get it, and Connie said, "I'm really sorry about this. I mean, with the hunk and all..."

"It's all right, Connie. Have a nice dinner and don't give this a second thought." She pushed the door open as the teenager returned with a duffel bag slung over her shoulder. "Come on in, Alison. We're pleased to have you."

The dog loped back into the living room, and Dana's toes started to tingle as the numbness began to fade. Still, she was careful about walking until she was certain her circulation was entirely restored.

Neither Zeke nor Tiffany had moved, but Dana noticed that Lou had come in from the kitchen and taken a seat on the arm of the couch as if to enjoy the show.

Tiffany consulted a tiny diamond-rimmed watch. "I must run. The supplier I'm meeting will be expecting me at the restaurant."

"Then I won't invite you to stay for pot roast," Zeke said cheerfully.

Dana seized the opening. "He made it especially for our house guest. Alison, I hope you don't mind sleeping on an air mattress on the floor. As you can see, we're not really set up for guests, but at least the bed is brand new—Zeke bought it today, just for you." She leveled a look at Zeke. "So you can stop telling Tiffany silly stories about why it's here. He's incorrigible, you know," she murmured to the blonde. "He just can't resist teasing."

"Silly stories?" Zeke sounded almost indignant. "I'm not the one who popped up with the whopper about the air mattress being a dog bed."

Dana's jaw dropped. As if it wasn't bad enough that she'd said it in the first place, now he had to go and repeat it. Was he *trying* to raise doubts in Tiffany's mind?

Dana plunged in. "Well, the way you were going on about me being ill, you were beginning to make me feel sick. Honestly, Zeke—"

Lou was grinning, Dana noticed. But surely she hadn't said anything funny...so what was the big joke?

"Of course you're not ill," Lou said fondly. "But you're not precisely well, either. I remember with my first, I was sick every morning for months. Oh, Dana—it's such wonderful news!"

He would send Connie flowers first thing in the morning, Zeke decided, as a token of thanks for bringing the houseguest.

He was grateful not because Alison's presence had helped to defuse the matter of the air mattress, but because Dana couldn't kill him in front of a witness. And it was quite obvious that she'd like to.

"I'll just go check on my pot roast again," he said as soon as Tiffany had retreated. "Lou, would you give me a hand in the kitchen?"

"Nothing much needs doing," Lou shrugged. "I finished up the salad and put it in the refrigerator while you were talking to that woman. And I turned the oven off so the potatoes and carrots wouldn't overcook. But I'd better be going home anyway to get my own dinner started.''

He was poking at the roast when Dana came into the kitchen and carefully closed the door behind her. ''Lou's gone?'' she said pleasantly enough, but she didn't wait for an answer. ''What in heaven's name inspired you to tell Tiffany I'm pregnant?''

''I didn't. You're the one who gave her the idea. And don't look at me as if you'd like to run me through the food chopper, Dana, because you can't ask the teenager to help you mop up the crime scene. It would be considered child abuse.''

''What do you mean, I'm the one who gave her the idea?''

Dana sounded a little odd, Zeke thought. Her teeth seemed to be clenched together. ''You said something about how before I knew it I'd be trading in the Jaguar for a minivan.''

''But how did she get from coaching a soccer team to the idea that there's already a kid on the way?''

''Actually, it was Lou who made that leap,'' Zeke said. ''She'd overheard the talk about you being under the weather, and she added the two things together.''

''And got sixteen. And you didn't correct her.''

''I thought there was no sense in confusing the situation.''

Dana shook her head. ''This whole thing wasn't already confused enough to suit you?''

''It seemed to do the trick where Tiffany was concerned, because that's when she started looking at her watch and talking about suppliers.''

''Have you forgotten that less than forty-eight hours ago, we were standing in the drawing room at Baron's Hill arguing about whether our divorce had ever become final?''

Zeke shrugged. ''So maybe you're only a little pregnant.''

Dana clamped both hands to her temples. She was making a noise that sounded to Zeke like a teakettle about to hit the boiling point.

''Besides,'' Zeke went on, ''Tiffany doesn't know we hadn't seen each other in years. As far as she's concerned this could have happened anytime in the last few weeks. I make at least one trip a month in this direction to talk to customers.''

Dana was looking at him in utter astonishment. "Dammit, Zeke, you're the one who keeps telling me what a small world it is. If anybody who was at Baron's Hill that night and overheard that discussion happens to be friends with Tiffany—"

"We were just putting on a show because you wanted to let Barclay down easy." He frowned. "No, I guess that explanation doesn't work very well. Come to think of it, maybe you're so upset because you are pregnant, but it doesn't have anything to do with me."

He watched her from the corner of his eye, fascinated by the play of emotion across her face. First puzzlement, then dawning awareness, and then a flash of rage that set him back on his heels. And he'd thought she'd been furious a few minutes ago...

This is a whole new level, Ferris. Watch your step.

She took a deep breath and started saying something in Chinese. It sounded to Zeke as if she was counting out loud, and if he was right, she was well past twenty before she got hold of herself and looked him straight in the eye. "Before you start believing your own stories, let's get this much straight—I'm not pregnant.''

''Sorry. I didn't mean to cast any aspersions on the sainted Barclay. I should have known he wouldn't take any risks.'' He watched her out of the corner of his eye. ''You know, I bet if you actually marry him, he'll make love to you every Saturday night. Regular as clockwork...and just about as exciting.''

He could see that Dana was biting her tongue, and he wondered what it was she wanted to say. Would she like to set him straight about Barclay's talents as a lover? Or announce that regular as clockwork was exactly what she wanted?

Not a chance, he thought. *Not my Dana.*

Their lovemaking had been every bit as much fun for her as it had been for him. And that was saying something. Unless, of course, she'd been faking that reaction the same way she'd pretended to like Polynesian food... But nobody could pretend the sort of enthusiasm his Dana had shown.

Only then did he realize what he'd been thinking. *My Dana...*

Better get hold of yourself, Ferris. And fast.

Zeke opened the oven door again and lifted the pan off the rack. "Do you want to tell the kid to wash up for dinner, or shall I?"

Dana pushed the kitchen door open. From the corner of his eye, Zeke saw a blur as the dog zoomed through the opening and past her. The animal's toenails clattered on the slick surface of the floor, scrambling for traction.

Dana fought to keep her balance as the dog slid around her and smacked into Zeke. Thrown sideways by the impact, he slammed into the sink and lost his grip. The pan flew out of his hands, rising in a gentle arc and then clanging to the floor, and as if in slow motion pot roast, carrots, onions, potatoes, and beef broth sprayed over the edge of the pan and pooled on the floor.

The dog lapped at the broth and pulled back with a whine as the hot liquid touched his tongue. But the scent obviously overwhelmed his caution and he began to gulp down the still-steaming food, nosing potatoes and carrots out of his way in order to tear chunks off the pot roast.

Alison came through the doorway. "Something smells really good in—" She stopped in midsentence. "I guess the dog thought it smelled good, too," she added lamely.

"Zeke believes in being efficient," Dana said. "Instead of giving the dog leftovers, he just feeds him first." She sounded suspiciously close to tears, Zeke thought—though he'd bet money she was actually trying with all her might not to laugh.

He seized the dog by the collar. "Come on, you stupid rhinoceros, you're not built to be a house dog."

Dana was wiping her eyes with a kitchen towel. "Oh, let him eat it, Zeke. If it was hot enough to actually hurt him, he'd back off."

"And spread out that way, it's cooling off fast," Alison noted. "The actual scientific process is called entropy and it means... Sorry, I guess I forgot the academic bowl is over for the day."

"Anybody for a burrito?" Dana asked brightly. "I'm buying."

Zeke and Alison started discussing entropy on the way to the restaurant, and by the time their food came, they were somewhere west of quantum physics. Dana, who'd been out of her depth within minutes, toyed with chips and salsa while she listened.

But one thing she had no trouble understanding was why the woman at the next table actually stopped to comment. "It's so unusual to see a young woman this age relating so well to her father," she gushed. "Hitting it off so well together, chatting and enjoying each other so much. How perfectly lovely!"

She swept on without waiting for a reply—which was just as well, Dana thought, because Zeke looked as if he'd swallowed a jalapeno whole.

"It's not you," Dana murmured to Alison. "It's just that he got a sudden taste of feeling his age and it gave him heartburn."

"I wish you were my dad, Zeke," Alison said suddenly. "Your kid's really going to be lucky, you know—having the two of you for parents."

Damn, Dana thought. Just when she'd almost managed to forget, up popped the fictional kid again. It was enough to make her long to order a shot of tequila, except that she was certain if she did, Alison would give her the entire lecture about why expectant mothers shouldn't drink. So she sipped her iced tea and glanced at Zeke, curious to see whether he was taking Alison's comment as a compliment or a threat.

He was frowning just a little and staring at a row of advertising posters on the far wall. *Threat,* Dana decided.

"I really wanted my parents to come to watch the academic bowl," Alison said. "But they're always too busy for that stuff. And I could never talk to my dad about things like entropy. He doesn't even *care* about why hot things don't stay hot." She dabbed her eyes with the corner of her napkin and then tossed it down. "Excuse me for a minute…"

She went off toward the ladies' room, and Zeke seemed to shake himself out of the funk he'd been lost in. "What was that all about?"

"Mostly it was about being sixteen and female," Dana said. "She'll be all right. Still, I'm glad she gave us a chance to talk. I assume you're going back to the hotel after dinner."

"With Tiffany in town? Don't be ridiculous."

"But you heard her, she's seeing a supplier tonight."

"You seriously think that's why she's here?"

"No," Dana said reluctantly. "I think she came to check on you." Maybe that fake-name business hadn't been as ridiculous as it had sounded after all. "I suppose I could take Alison and check in somewhere, but—"

"Same objection applies. If Tiffany saw your name in a hotel register, we'd be dead."

"I don't think we're doing all that well as it is." She stabbed a tomato chunk that had fallen out of her taco. "You know, Zeke, if you were going to adopt an animal, you should have made it a pit bull. Then she'd never have gotten as far as the front door and we wouldn't be in this mess."

"It's not the dog's fault."

Dana sniffed. "The only thing the rhino will attack is pot roast."

"Well, to be fair, if it had been an ordinary burglar he would probably have gone for the throat. But since it was Tiffany—even a pit bull would have cowered in fear."

"She looks like a fluff ball."

"That's what makes her dangerous."

A man loomed over the table. "Zeke Ferris! I haven't seen you since you moved out of the Quagmire."

The Quagmire. How very long it had been since Dana had heard that phrase.

"It must have been about the time you graduated. Remember me? Ned Marsh. I hear you struck it big along the way."

Zeke got to his feet. "Hello, Ned. You know Dana, of course?"

"The reason he moved out of the Quagmire," Dana said, and offered her hand.

"Oh, heck, yes," Ned crowed. "I'll never forget that blind date, because I'm the one who got you two together."

In a manner of speaking, Dana thought.

But Ned Marsh wasn't even looking at Dana; his attention was focused tightly on Zeke. "Look, you sort of owe me a favor for that, don't you think? I understand you're selling out your company."

"Word does spread quickly," Zeke murmured.

"I thought if I could get a little piece of the action…"

"You want to buy some stock just in time to sell it at a profit, you mean?"

"People do it all the time," Ned pointed out stiffly.

"With publicly held companies, I suppose. But this one is privately owned. There isn't any stock to sell to you."

Ned sounded a little affronted. "Privately owned by you, you mean. You could find a way to cut me in if you wanted to."

This isn't going to be pretty, Dana thought as she watched Zeke's face. She hoped Alison didn't come back in the middle of it; not only would the girl lose her respect for Zeke, but she might learn a few new words, too.

Zeke pulled a sleek leather folder from the inside pocket of his jacket. "Here's my number, Ned. Call me at the office next week."

Ned's fingers closed avariciously around Zeke's business card. "Thanks, pal. You bet I'll call!" He hurried away, almost knocking Alison aside in his rush.

Zeke sat down again, and Dana looked at him thoughtfully over her iced tea glass. "You aren't going to be in the office next week."

"Oh, you never know," Zeke said absently. "I might be."

"But you aren't going to make a deal with Ned, are you? You don't owe him anything."

He grinned suddenly. "You heard him, Dana. I owe him for getting us together."

"Ouch." Dana reached for the bill. "Maybe I should have warned the poor guy that you think of that as an entirely different sort of debt than he does."

Setting up the air mattress required pushing every piece of furniture in the living room tightly against the walls and smashing the curtains on the front windows against the glass. And even then one corner of the mattress extended under the small table by the kitchen door. Dana surveyed the results with resignation.

"Last call for midnight snacks," Zeke murmured to Dana. "Because if you wait till midnight you'll have to step on Alison to get to the kitchen. Or, for that matter, to get to the front door, the back door, or the bathroom."

It wasn't quite as bad as he made it sound, but Dana knew exactly what he meant. With the teenager's bed set up, the two of them were unable to move freely. In effect, they were isolated together in Dana's bedroom.

"It does bring back old memories," Zeke said cheerfully. "That apartment we lived in wasn't much bigger than this bed. What do you need a king-size bed for, anyway?"

"It isn't king-size, it just looks big because the room's so small."

Zeke kicked off his shoes and lay down on top of the quilt. "You're right," he said. "I don't even have to stretch for my toes to touch the footboard."

"Hey, that quilt's an antique. Turn it back, don't lie on top of it."

"Darling," he said huskily. "I didn't dare hope that you'd invite me under the covers, but if you'd really like—"

"I'd really like to throw you out the window. Or give you a pile of blankets so you could sleep on the floor."

"There's no floor to sleep on," Zeke pointed out. He rose lazily.

"I'm aware of that." Dana pulled the quilt off and folded it neatly over the back of the room's single straight chair. Still fully clothed, she settled on one edge of the bed, propping herself up with pillows. "So it looks as if we're stuck with each other for the night. Don't let me keep you from enjoying the television." She tossed the remote control at him and reached for her book.

Zeke lay down and squinted at the tiny television, mounted on a bracket high on the wall above the footboard. "You forgot the binoculars," he muttered.

Dana pretended to ignore him. It was no easy task. Standing up, he seemed to fill the whole living room. In the forced intimacy of the much smaller bedroom, sprawled across her bed, he seemed to be invading every inch of her life.

Don't think about it, she told herself. *It's only one night. You can make it through.*

"Running into Ned Marsh was what really brought back memories," she mused. "I'd almost blocked out the memory of the Quagmire. I wonder if it's still there."

The Quagmire. The old house on the wrong side of the worst street anywhere near campus. The house where Zeke had been living when she met him, on the night she'd had the infamous blind date with Ned Marsh.

Ned hadn't set up the date, he'd *been* the date. He'd walked over to the dormitory to meet her, and then he'd remembered that he'd left his wallet behind. So they'd walked back to the house so he could get it, and he'd invited Dana to come in with him. She'd flipped a mental coin—was it more dangerous to go inside a house full of guys with a man she didn't know, or to wait on the sidewalk in a frankly terrifying neighborhood?—and she'd opted for inside. And it was while she was waiting in the foyer—or what would have been the foyer if it hadn't been piled with everything from coats to skis to tennis racquets to garbage bags—that Zeke had come in.

She'd been standing on the bottom step, reading the messages scrawled on the oatmeal-colored wallpaper on the stairwell, when the door opened. Caution made her look over her shoulder—and fascination make her keep looking.

His hair had been longer then, and his clothes would have been turned down by any self-respecting thrift store. But there was something about the way he carried himself which said this man stepped aside for someone only when he chose to.

He'd hung his threadbare backpack from the newel post, which seemed to be the only place which wasn't already piled a foot deep, and stood still to look Dana over from head to toe. "What brings you to the Quagmire?" he'd said, and she'd told him she was with Ned Marsh.

He said soberly, "I don't think that's a very good idea."

Just then Ned had come down the stairs, dodging piles and laughing self-consciously. "I guess we can't go to the movie after all," he said. "I forgot to pay my rent, and Joe just nailed me for it. So the cupboard's bare, honey. But we can watch television in my room."

"No, thanks," Dana said coolly. "If you'll walk me back to my dorm—"

Ned had argued, and Zeke had calmly told him to dry up and he'd walked Dana home himself. On the way, he'd told her about the Quagmire—so named because things and even people could disappear into its depths and not be found for days. And he'd told her that whoever had set her up for a blind date with Ned Marsh had done her no favor at all.

Dana wasn't so sure she agreed. A couple of days later, when Zeke called to invite her to half-price night at the local diner, she'd been even more inclined to think he was wrong. And three weeks after that, when he'd proposed...

I should have run away screaming. Instead, she'd helped scrape together enough money to rent an efficiency apartment and pay for a license and a judge, and she'd married him. And three months later—with graduation looming, job hunts hanging over their heads, and stress magnifying their disagreements, they had indulged in one final, spectacular fight...and they had parted.

"I doubt it," Zeke said.

Caught off guard, Dana stared at him. "You doubt what?"

"I was answering your question," he said impatiently. "I said I doubt that the Quagmire's still there."

"Oh. Of course. No, it couldn't be—not the shape it was in. How many guys lived there, anyway? I never did get a head count."

"Nobody else did, either, except maybe Joe who collected the rent. A dozen maybe. Sometimes more. Especially 'round the end of the semester, when money was particularly tight, the place would be full of sleeping bags." The subject seemed to hold little interest for him.

"It almost sounded tonight as if Ned Marsh was trying to blackmail you."

Zeke turned his head to look at her. "And you're wondering what it is he's holding over my head, aren't you?"

"I didn't say that. I just said it sounded as if—"

"Have fun thinking about it. Sweet dreams, honey." He flicked the remote, and the television died.

Dana tried to read a little longer, but her book might as well have been printed in hieroglyphs. Finally she put it down and turned off the light.

Zeke's breathing was light and steady, as if he had not a care in the world. But Dana's heart felt jumpy. She couldn't help reliving the last night they'd spent together, after that final, horrendous fight. Then, too, there had been no extra space, and so they had shared a bed—but nothing else at all. Not a word, not a touch.

In utter exhaustion she had finally fallen asleep, and in the morning all that was left of her marriage was a terse note Zeke had left to tell her that he was moving back into the Quagmire.

It was almost hilarious, she thought, that the one time she didn't want to know about his plans, he had punctiliously left her a note....

Eventually, as she had on the last night of their marriage, she slept. And she dreamed—a deeply erotic dream. The kind she had frequently had in the first year after their split. A dream in which she was with him once more, sharing body and soul with a hunger which no other act could ease.

This time it wasn't a note which greeted her at dawn. It was a sleep-roughened voice which said directly into her ear, "If you're looking for trouble, sweetheart, you're just about to find it."

CHAPTER SEVEN

DANA'S eyes snapped open as if he'd touched a spring—so fast and so wide, Zeke thought ruefully, that she couldn't possibly have faked the reaction.

It wasn't the first time in his life that he'd regretted his mother teaching him to act like a gentleman, but this was easily the least convenient. If he'd only been able to ignore his conscience... After all, he wasn't the one who'd wrapped her body around his like a warm coat on a winter's day—Dana had done that all by herself. He'd simply awakened to find himself flat on his back with a warm and willing woman draped over him.

Warm, willing, but—even with her eyes open now—obviously still asleep.

Dana stared at him from a distance of less than three inches, blinked, and tried again to focus. He watched as comprehension dawned in her eyes, followed rapidly by dismay as she realized the position she was in. ''Oh, no,'' she said. ''You're not getting by with this.''

His jaw dropped. "Why in hell are you blaming me? If I was trying to take advantage of the situation, it would already be way too late for you to protest." And after a couple of minutes of the sort of treatment he had in mind, he'd bet she wouldn't even want to protest. The thought made his mouth go dry. "If you insist on melting over me like butter on toast—" He was hot enough to melt her, that was sure. Everywhere she was touching him, he felt scorched—even through two layers of clothes.

Color flooded her face as she scrambled to free herself.

Zeke's arms tightened around her, holding her face close to his. "Just remember one thing, Dana. You've used up your get-out-of-jail-free card. Next time I refuse to be responsible for the consequences."

"There won't be a next time," she snapped.

That's a darn shame. Zeke let her go.

Dana slithered away and sat up on the edge of the bed, arms folded across her chest, trembling. With fear? Surely not. With anger? More likely. With embarrassment?

Bingo.

"That," she said, "was entirely uncalled for." Even her voice was shaky.

Zeke was beginning to feel grumpy. He hadn't even *done* anything. Well, all right, he hadn't been in any big hurry to wake her up—he'd been curious about how far she'd go. But he could have taken her up on that sensual and nonverbal invitation without bothering to ask himself if she really meant it. Didn't he get any credit at all for restraint?

"Look, Dana, you might try to remember that I'm not exactly desperate here. There are enough women who like the idea of having me in their beds that I don't have to force myself on the unwilling ones." He added thoughtfully, "Not that you appeared to be reluctant for a while there, but—"

She stood up and stalked over to pull open the bedroom door. He fully expected that she'd slam it behind her. Instead, she stopped dead in the doorway as if she'd run into an invisible wall.

Too curious to ignore her, and too irritated to remain lounging on her bed, he followed her. She jerked away as he came up behind her. "We have got to work on those jitters of yours,'' he murmured, and looked past her into the living room.

In the center of the air mattress lay not only Alison, still fast asleep, but the dog, who had tucked himself into the bend of the teenager's knees with his chin propped on her ankles. He opened one eye and gave a gentle, warning woof.

Dana eyed Zeke. ''I thought you put him on the back porch last night.''

''I did.''

Alison stretched, yawned, and sat up. ''He didn't like it out there, so I let him come in.''

''He probably wanted to make sure nobody had dropped anything on the kitchen floor while he was gone,'' Dana said.

''He was lonely.'' Alison patted the dog's head and he tried to grin at her and to lick her chin.

''Want to take him home with you, Alison?'' Dana asked. She sounded hopeful, Zeke thought. ''He seems to have gotten attached to you.''

''Are you kidding? My mother would have a stroke.''

''I was afraid of that.'' Dana sighed. ''I don't think the radio announcements are going to work, Zeke. We need some posters put up around the neighborhood—that'll give you something to do today. We could offer a reward.''

He started to tell her that he'd already planned his day before what she'd said sank in. ''A reward? But we're the ones who found him. The owners pay the reward.''

''Look, it's worth a couple of hundred to me if anyone will claim him. I don't care whether it's his real owners—I'll pay anyone who'll take him away. Alison, the academic bowl starts in an hour. If you'd like the shower first, I'll fix breakfast.''

''Just as long as there's nothing citrus.'' Alison popped to her feet. ''I'm allergic to it.''

The dog looked mournfully after her and then put his head down on the warm spot where her feet had rested.

''*Now* he decides to be a guard dog,'' Dana muttered.

Zeke had no trouble interpreting the look she gave him. He put the dog out the front door, over the animal's protests, and went back to the kitchen. The drip in the kitchen faucet appeared to have grown worse overnight. He wouldn't be surprised if it broke loose entirely before the day was out. He wondered if Dana knew what an off-hours house call by a plumber cost.

"My favorite French toast recipe calls for orange juice." Dana broke eggs into a shallow bowl and reached past him to get a fork. "Zeke, what are we going to do?"

"Make pancakes instead."

"I wasn't talking about food. What about Tiffany? I don't think she was impressed."

That's the understatement of the year. "I warned you it would take a while to convince her. If telling her would have done it, I wouldn't be here at all."

The way she sighed left no doubt how she felt about that. It was a good thing he didn't still cherish any long-term illusions about the two of them, Zeke thought, because if he had, the weight of that sigh would have bruised his ego pretty thoroughly.

"Isn't there anything we can do to speed it up?"

Zeke looked her over thoughtfully and mused, "I could invite her over for breakfast. It would be very good timing if she saw you right about now."

"Why?"

"Because with those dark circles under your eyes you look as if you're suffering from terminal morning sickness. She couldn't help but be impressed."

She threw an egg at him.

Zeke fielded it like a softball and handed it back. "I have an even better idea than pancakes."

"You want something else, make it yourself. I'm not a short-order cook."

He waited silently until she turned to look at him, so he could see her reaction. "Give the kid a few bucks to buy herself breakfast at the cafeteria, and we can go back to bed and finish what you started."

Now that she was fully awake she had much more self-control, because she didn't start sputtering as he'd half expected she would. "I thought you said you weren't desperate enough to sleep with me."

Interesting way to put it. "No, I said you weren't my only option. It's an entirely different thing."

"If you say so." She didn't sound convinced. "And what exactly do you think would change if I slept with you?"

"Not much where Tiffany's concerned," he admitted, "but I'd feel a whole lot better and so would you."

For an instant, she looked as if she was actually considering the suggestion, and Zeke felt his breath catch.

"You don't really want to do that," she said finally.

Yes, I do. He could still feel the imprint of her body against his, still feel her softness and her warmth. "I don't?"

Dana shook her head. "I might have such a good time that I forgot how much I've enjoyed being divorced from you," she said gently. "And then—poor guy—you'd be stuck with me all over again."

She'd managed to pull herself together in the end, but Dana had never been so mortified in her life. It wasn't just the dream that embarrassed her—nobody had control of their dreams, for heaven's sake. It wasn't even the way her subconscious had ignored the facts and gone straight for the feelings, as if all the years and bitter words and harsh emotions had never intervened.

It was how she'd reacted after Zeke woke her up that was so disconcerting. Why hadn't she just laughed it off? Why had she sat there on the edge of the bed acting like a threatened virgin?

She'd set herself up for Zeke's invitation, that was sure. *We can go back to bed and finish what you started.* She'd handed him a perfect win-win situation, and he hadn't hesitated to exploit the possibilities. If she turned him down, he'd have the fun of watching her get flustered. And if she didn't turn him down...

Well, nobody had ever said Zeke Ferris was an angel.

Opportunist is more like it, she told herself. If she'd shown any interest at all, he'd probably have bundled Alison out of the house even if she was wearing only a bath towel. And then...

Dana could feel herself growing warm at the thought.

As soon as Alison reappeared, Zeke took over the griddle and Dana went to take a shower. He was right, she moaned as she looked in the mirror. She did look gaunt and ill.

I'm not exactly desperate, he'd said. But—judging by what she saw in her mirror—Dana wasn't so sure. If he found her inviting under these circumstances, he sounded pretty desperate to her.

When she returned to the living room, the air mattress was back in its box, the table had been pulled out from the wall, and Zeke and Alison were eating French toast. Zeke pulled the low swivel chair over from Dana's desk to the table and shifted his plate in order to leave a place for her.

"We'll be getting the house ready to sell," he told Alison earnestly. "It's just not big enough for three of us."

Quite true, Dana thought. Also extremely misleading, but there was no point in trying to correct Alison's mistaken impression now. So she sat down and put two slices of French toast on her plate.

Zeke raised an eyebrow at her. "You must be feeling better this morning."

Dana refused to be drawn into a discussion of her supposed illness. "I'm fine, thank you."

"Honey, you've got incredible grit," Zeke murmured. "I'm so proud of you. Whenever you two are ready, I'll take you over to the university.''

Alison brightened. ''Are you coming to watch the academic bowl?''

''No, but I'll drop you off on my way to the home-supply store. I need to get a new faucet for the kitchen sink before that leak turns into Old Faithful. Do you want a modern style or a reproduction, Dana?''

''Actually,'' Dana said pleasantly, ''I'd rather keep the current one.''

Alison took her empty plate and Zeke's to the kitchen.

Zeke leaned back in the swivel chair with his coffee mug cupped in one hand. ''Well, I guess it wouldn't be the first drip you've grown attached to,'' he murmured. ''Take Barclay, for example—''

''Don't change the subject. I didn't ask you to fix my faucet, Zeke. In fact, I don't *want* you to fix my faucet.''

''I suppose next you'll be telling me to make the gutter sag again.''

''Well, I'm not quite that much of a masochist,'' Dana admitted. ''But I'd rather you give some thought to the Tiffany problem.''

"Trust me, I've been thinking." He looked up as Alison came back. "Is your bag packed?"

The dog was waiting patiently on the front step. He escorted them to the Jaguar and bounced inside when Zeke opened the door. Dana tried, without much success, to bite back a smile at the look on his face.

"Oh, let him come," she urged. "You wouldn't want to leave the rhino here feeling abandoned. He might be so upset he'd run away."

Zeke dragged the dog out of the car and put Alison's bag in the back seat. She hugged the animal and climbed in.

Between the regular weekday traffic and the academic bowl, there was no place to park anywhere near Dressler Hall.

"This is why I walk to work," Dana said. "Just pull over by the front door and we'll get out."

Instead Zeke circled the parking lot again. As if by magic, a space opened and he slid the Jaguar into it. "I'll carry Alison's bag inside. I'm morally certain her mother doesn't want her exerting herself, and I don't want you overdoing things right now, either, Dana."

He sounded very solicitous, Dana thought. Almost paternal, in fact. Dana bit her tongue to keep from pointing that out.

Students were milling around the main foyer of Dressler Hall, checking the bulletin boards for their room assignments and waiting for the start of the first round. Professor Wells was standing at the foot of the stairway, a copy of the room list in one hand, fielding questions. In the middle of the hallway, working the crowd, was Barclay.

Dana hadn't invited him to be a part of the academic bowl, but she supposed she should have expected him to show up anyway, because Barclay wouldn't miss an opportunity to recruit a student—and these high school kids would be choosing colleges in a year or two.

He was shaking hands quickly and efficiently, introducing himself and apparently listening with full concentration to each young person. But—now that she knew what to look for—Dana could see his gaze roving over the crowd, choosing his next target and the one after that. He probably wasn't hearing a single word any of them said.

Barclay's gaze came to rest on Dana and then flicked to Zeke. Within moments he'd freed himself from the throng and came striding across the foyer. "You're leaving?" he asked, and pointed at the duffel Zeke was carrying. "You've got a bag."

"Now imagine you noticing that," Zeke said gently. "All by yourself and everything."

Alison giggled, took the bag, and went off to join her teammates.

Barclay's smile was the biggest Dana had ever seen. She felt foreboding creep over her. Would he remember the promise she'd extracted from him, or would he go off like a loose cannon? If he started in on Zeke about making a donation...

"There's someone I want you to meet, Dana," Barclay said eagerly. He looked over the heads of the crowd. "She's here somewhere...just a little thing, easy to lose."

He's talking about a prospective student, Dana told herself. But she felt a cold trickle of foreboding creep down her spine.

The chattering students began to move off in groups toward their assigned rooms, and through the thinning throng in the foyer Dana saw Mrs. Janowitz and Professor Wells talking to a petite blonde who had her back turned to the door.

A petite, fluffy-looking blonde wearing a suit that Dana knew was exactly the same icy-blue color as her eyes. Even from the back, she knew who it was—Tiffany Rowe, in the flesh.

The cold trickle in Dana's back hardened into an iceberg.

"I'm sure you've heard the name," Barclay said eagerly. "After all, there's Rowe Library, Rowe Auditorium, Rowe Center for the Performing Arts, Rowe Law School..."

"You mean here?" Dana hardly recognized her own voice, for it was little more than a squeak.

Zeke shot a look at her as if to say that had been the stupidest question he'd ever heard.

And he was right, Dana admitted. She knew perfectly well what the university library was called, and the law school, too—and neither of them had been named after a donor named Rowe. Nevertheless, suddenly she was doubting herself.

And she was beginning to understand the effect Tiffany Rowe could have. No wonder Zeke didn't want to work for her.

"Oh, no," Barclay assured her. "The Rowe buildings are scattered at universities all over the country. Some of the very best universities.''

''And Tiffany did all that?'' Dana felt as if there were a python squeezing her chest, keeping her from breathing properly.

Barclay chuckled. ''Well, not personally. She's not old enough, for one thing—some of those buildings have been around for a hundred years. But now that she's taking an interest in this university, surely she'll be asking the family foundation to consider us.''

''Gee, I wonder what brought on the sudden interest in this particular university,'' Zeke said under his breath.

Barclay drew himself up a little straighter, but he still had to look up a couple of inches at Zeke. ''Well, I'd say that's obvious. Ever since I've been here, we've had wonderful ratings and reviews. There have been articles about our programs and our innovations. Of course she became aware of what we're doing here at the university, just as every other forward-thinking business person in the country has learned about us.'' He smiled modestly. ''And though I don't like to brag, I think the personal factor enters into it, as well. Tiffany and I hit it off extremely well, the moment we met last night.''

No doubt, Dana thought. *You have so much in common—like refusing to take no for an answer.* ''And how did you happen to meet?''

Barclay seemed startled by the question. ''She called me.''

''Out of the blue?''

He sounded almost defensive. ''We have mutual acquaintances. A local industrialist who's a member of the university's board, for one.''

Tiffany said she was meeting with a supplier last night, Dana thought wryly. *But she didn't say exactly what she expected him to supply.*

But why had she wanted an introduction to Barclay? Exactly what did Tiffany suspect— and what was she trying to find out?

''I asked her to come this morning to watch the academic bowl. It's really a shame we don't have anything more exciting going on this week.''

''If I'd only known,'' Dana said, ''I'd have done my best to bring in a circus.''

Barclay obviously wasn't listening. ''I'm going to get her,'' he said. ''Mrs. Janowitz has taken up enough of Tiffany's time, and Mary

Wells had better get this competition started or it'll go on all weekend.'' He walked off briskly.

"And you said *my* ego was the size of a continent,'' Zeke murmured. "It's enough to make me wonder how this university survived for a century and a half before he came on board. It must have been on life support."

"Did you know about this? The Rowe Foundation, I mean, and whatever all those buildings were."

Zeke shook his head. "It's a pretty common name," he pointed out. "And I've never met any of Tiffany's family. Judging by her, though, major philanthropy would be the last thing I'd expect from them."

"I don't think you're likely to see any self-less sacrifice now, either."

Dana watched the tableau as Barclay approached the two women, touching Mrs. Janowitz on the shoulder. She stepped aside to invite him into the circle. He said something and three feminine heads turned in their direction. Professor Wells waved casually and strode off toward the stairs, carrying the locked briefcase containing the morning's contest questions. Mrs. Janowitz looked disappointed at being interrupted. Tiffany didn't even twitch an eyebrow.

"But what does she want?" Dana asked helplessly. "Why is she here? Is she just checking up on me in general, or does she want something else altogether?"

"Maybe, if we're really lucky, she'll decide she wants Barclay. Sorry, Dana, but some sacrifice on your part may be required."

"Like I haven't already paid the price," Dana muttered.

What she wanted, Tiffany assured Dana earnestly when Barclay brought her over, was to help in the education of the young people. She was delighted to pitch in, and since her new friend Mrs. Janowitz was feeling a little worn down after the stresses of the previous day, Tiffany would be happy to step in and assist the older woman.

Dana interpreted that to mean that Tiffany wasn't volunteering to do the actual work, she just wanted an excuse to hang around and observe. But with Barclay standing by and grinning, Dana could hardly turn down Tiffany's offer. She certainly couldn't accuse the woman of having ulterior motives.

She couldn't even separate her from Mrs. Janowitz, because Tiffany had phrased her offer so carefully. But if Mrs. Janowitz had the opportunity to share her grievances over the way that Dana had, in her opinion, led Barclay on only to dump him when her husband reappeared....

"I'm sure Mrs. Janowitz will be pleased to have your help," Dana said. Her voice didn't even crack; she was quite proud of herself. "I'll take you up to the room—"

"Oh, no, my dear." Tiffany sounded shocked. "I'm sure someone else can do that. You must conserve your strength." Her cool blue gazed summed Dana up. "You look simply awful this morning."

Dana managed to keep her voice level. "Thanks so much for your sympathy. You have no idea how much I appreciate it."

Barclay beamed. "You're so thoughtful of others, Tiffany. Goodbye, everybody—I must get back to my office and take care of whatever crises have hit while I've been gone."

Tiffany didn't wait for him to be out of earshot. "I feel so sorry for you," she went on. "Until today, I had no idea morning sickness could do so much damage to a woman."

Mrs. Janowitz gasped. "Morning sickness?"

Tiffany looked coolly at her. "Oh, didn't you know? Dana's pregnant...or at least she says she is."

I never said anything of the sort, Dana wanted to shout. She smiled instead, but her lips hurt. "You'll be in room twelve this morning. Professor Wells will bring in the question packets as soon as you're settled."

Tiffany climbed the stairs with her head high. Mrs. Janowitz looked as if she had to drag herself up them, and she kept looking back at Dana as if in shock.

"You know," Zeke said, "I'm beginning to think Barclay and Tiffany may be a match made in heaven. It's too bad for you, of course, but you really can't blame him, Dana. Look at the opportunities she could open up for him."

"That's wishful thinking," she said absently.

Not that he was exactly wrong, she thought. Barclay would go for it in a minute—Dana hadn't forgotten him confiding that he had no intention of spending his entire career at a small private university. Tiffany, with her influence at the universities which already boasted Rowe Library, Rowe Law School, Rowe Auditorium, and all the rest, was Barclay's dream girl, no doubt of that.

But as for the idea that Tiffany would fall for someone like Barclay...there wasn't a chance in the world of that. She was far too manipulative and controlling herself not to see him for exactly what he was—shallow, vain, and self-promoting. Besides, how could any woman who had the basic good sense to want Zeke ever bring herself to settle for Barclay?

It was no more than a passing rumination, and in fact for a minute it hardly caused a ripple in Dana's conscious thought process. But when she finally realized what she'd been thinking, she felt as if she'd run smack into a tree.

Since when was it *basic good sense* for a woman to want Zeke?

She scrambled to justify the idea. It wasn't as if Barclay provided any serious competition. There wasn't anything so terribly special about Zeke, it was just that Barclay was nowhere in the same class. Of course, on a list of desirable companions, Barclay fell considerably below the rhino—so thinking that any woman with a brain would prefer Zeke to Barclay was no big compliment to Zeke.

It was certainly a relief to have that figured out.

"I hope your day gets better," Zeke said.

He was almost out the door by the time Dana pulled herself together. "Oh, no, you don't, buddy. You're not going to escape to the home-supply store. You get up to room twelve and keep an eye on Tiffany. Don't let her have a heart-to-heart chat with Mrs. Janowitz."

Zeke looked as though he was prepared to make a run for it. "Look, I know you said you didn't want a new faucet, but you can't hold me prisoner, Dana."

Dana added firmly, "If you abandon me, I'll make a deal with Tiffany."

He stopped. "What kind of a deal? Not that I'm worried, you understand, just curious."

"Right—you're not worried. Here's the deal. I will remove myself from her path so she can hunt you down at her leisure, and *she* pays for the conference center." Dana shrugged. "You see, I don't care whose money builds it, as long as it gets built. So if you want to save yourself seven and a half million dollars, Zeke, walk out that door. I dare you.''

Zeke didn't walk out. Doing his best to look meek, he went up to room twelve, where he slouched in a student desk at the back and watched Alison's team stomp on their first competition of the morning.

But he wasn't paying much attention to the questions. He was musing about what Dana had said.

She hadn't even reacted to the suggestion that Barclay might slip away from her and into Tiffany's pocket while Dana was otherwise occupied—except to comment that in her opinion Zeke was indulging in wishful thinking.

But was she really so unconcerned? Did she have such excellent control of herself, to be able to pretend that didn't bother her, if it actually did? He doubted it, considering how she'd reacted this morning when she'd awakened to find herself in an embarrassingly intimate embrace. That woman hadn't shown anything like rigid self-control then.

Though now that he came to think of it, why had she reacted so strongly this morning? It wasn't as if she'd never been in that position before. He couldn't begin to remember how many times she'd seduced him, so she couldn't have been embarrassed over the action itself. Besides, they'd both been fully clothed this morning, so she hadn't exactly been in any danger, either from him or from herself. Houdini would have had trouble extracting her from her clothes in that position.

And yet she'd been so nervous about finding herself in bed with him that she'd stammered and trembled and made crazy accusations. *Because of what Barclay would think if he found out*, Zeke told himself.

But the answer wasn't satisfying, because he would bet his soul that what had happened this morning had nothing to do with Barclay. For one thing, Barclay was so self-centered, so pompous, so arrogant that it would never cross his mind to wonder if the woman he wanted could actually feel desire for another man. That truth wouldn't dawn on Barclay even if he stumbled across them making love in the foyer of Dressler Hall.

And that, Zeke thought, was an idea that certainly had its attractions....

He tugged his mind back to the matter at hand.

Whatever else Dana was, she was honest with herself. She might consider marrying Barclay because she liked the idea of being first lady of the university—but she couldn't pretend that she was in love with him. She might choose a partner who held no passionate attraction, because passion hadn't been enough to save her marriage last time—but she would know what was missing. She might choose to overlook Barclay's idiosyncracies, but she wouldn't deny them.

No, she hadn't pulled away from him this morning because she was afraid of Barclay's reaction. She'd been afraid because she still felt the magic she and Zeke had shared. It had scared her to realize that subconsciously, she still desired him—and she had panicked.

She still wanted him. She showed it every time he came near her, in the way she shied from his touch. And there was no denying that a couple of days in her company had reawakened Zeke's desires, too.

The marriage hadn't worked out—but divorcing hadn't killed the passion they had shared. It had flickered down like an abandoned campfire until flames no longer showed. But underneath, the embers were still hot, and with the right kindling and just a breath from a bellows, it would come to life once more. It might even burn hotter than before.

And if that happened, then—as far as he was concerned—Tiffany could take her own sweet time.

CHAPTER EIGHT

Despite Dana's earlier fears about the capacity of the auditorium, all of the contestants in the academic bowl managed to crowd in late that afternoon to watch as the winners' trophies were presented. Professor Wells read off the names of the winning teams, and Dana handed out the awards—miniature loving cups for each individual member and a larger version for the team's school. She was particularly delighted when Alison's name was called as part of the second-prize team.

"We'll see you all next year," Professor Wells said. The crowd roared and from scattered spots all over the auditorium kids waved silvery loving cups in the air.

Barclay applauded along with the rest, from his seat on the stage, but before the noise had died down he approached the podium. "Just a few final thoughts," he said. "Professor Wells and Ms. Mulholland have done their usual great job, but I have just a few things I want to add."

Dana smothered a groan. With an auditorium packed to bursting with kids who'd been cooped up for two days and chaperones who were eager to get their charges home, Barclay wanted to give an impromptu speech?

What was it Connie had said about him? *He does like to hear himself talk,* that was it.

Amazing, Dana thought, that it had taken her so long to notice something which had been so obvious to Connie. That was one thing to thank Zeke for, at least—he'd kept her from making that colossal mistake....

She frowned. Where had that thought come from? Why was she crediting Zeke? He hadn't saved her from anything—not from Barclay, and certainly not from her own shortsighted attraction to the man. Long before Zeke had come on the scene, she'd seen through Barclay.

Well, maybe not *long* before. But a few hours was as good as a year. As long as she'd seen the truth before it had been too late to back out, what difference did it make exactly when she'd realized what Barclay really was?

Zeke did make it easier to break free, though, she admitted. Whether it was her supposedly-revived marriage or—more likely—

the possible major contribution she'd dangled over his head, Barclay had gotten the message loud and clear. And Tiffany's appearance on the scene had successfully distracted him from both Dana and the major contribution. Yes, Zeke had made things easier.

She applauded politely along with the rest of the crowd as Barclay adjusted the microphone and cleared his throat. But she wasn't listening; her gaze was roving the hall. Zeke was still there, near the back surrounded by Alison's team. But where was Tiffany? He was supposed to be keeping an eye on her. Had she finally given up and gone away?

The noise level in the auditorium was creeping higher as the kids grew more restless.

"And I have every confidence," Barclay was almost shouting, "that by next year, when you return to take part in the academic bowl again, we'll be welcoming you to an entirely new conference center here on campus."

Dana gulped. A year? What made him so sure they could raise the rest of the funds that quickly? Barclay couldn't possibly know about the deal she'd struck with Zeke. He'd obviously latched onto her hint and was hoping for a major contribution—but what had made him assume Zeke wouldn't have his own ideas about how his money should be spent?

Her common sense kicked in once more. Of course Barclay didn't know; he had to be speaking generally, talking about the ongoing campaign to raise funds and his confidence that they'd be able to pull it off soon. It was only her own slightly guilty conscience that had made her think Barclay was referring to anything more specific.

"I am confident," Barclay went on, "that through the generosity of a completely new donor—one we've never been honored to work with before—we'll be able to build a state-of-the-art center that's just as terrific as all of you young people who'll be using it."

Zeke's going to kill me, Dana thought.

"Of course, until it's all official I can't tell you exactly what the center will be called," he said, "but we'll be naming it after the donor." He grinned broadly. "And I can tell you this— you won't find the name hard to remember."

Dana realized with a surge of relief that Barclay wasn't looking at either her or Zeke. She followed his gaze and saw that he was looking straight at Tiffany Rowe. Dana hadn't spotted her earlier because there was a whole basketball team—or at least a group of guys who were tall enough to be—sitting right in front of her.

He's announcing the Rowe Conference Center. I wonder if Tiffany's made a promise or Barclay only thinks she has.

"That's all the wisdom I have to share today," Barclay finished. "Come back and see us again, all of you!"

"Wisdom, he calls it," Professor Wells snorted as she came up to Dana. "What was all that nonsense about? Who on earth does he think is going to come up with that kind of money all in one chunk?" She didn't wait for an answer. "I am never again volunteering to take on something like this. How you do it day after day is beyond me, Dana. And you've got Baron's Hill to manage, too."

"That reminds me," Dana said. "Barclay's having a dinner party tomorrow, and I haven't had a chance to check back with the caterers or the florist or the string quartet. If even one of them doesn't come through as they promised, I'm toast."

Professor Wells gave her a sympathetic smile and melted into the crowd. Dana saw her a couple of minutes later at the doorway, saying goodbye to the departing teams.

As soon as Barclay had left the podium, Dana turned off the sound system and began to unplug and roll up cords and cables. She was fitting the microphone back into its protective case when Alison bounded onto the stage.

"We're leaving now," the teenager said. "Can I have a hug? I wanted one when you gave me my trophy, but I didn't think it would look right—people might think you'd been playing favorites."

"They can't think that now," Dana said, and held the girl close for a long moment. "Come and visit me if you're back on campus, Alison."

The teenager grinned. "I want to come and see your baby."

A snort from behind her made Dana turn. Mrs. Janowitz was standing on the steps to the stage.

Dana gave Alison a final hug and promised, feeling like a world-class fraud, to send her a birth announcement. She'd have to write a letter, she reminded herself, telling the teenager the truth. But she simply couldn't explain in front of Mrs. Janowitz—it would be like broadcasting the news via the local emergency-siren system.

The girl hurried off to rejoin her teammates, and Dana raised an eyebrow at Mrs. Janowitz. "You were going to say something?"

"Baby indeed," the woman sniffed. "Under the circumstances, I can't help but wonder if you even know who the father is. Leading Barclay on as you did, and then *this*—"

Dana hadn't expected the attack to come from exactly that direction, and it took her a second to get her breath back. "Mrs. Janowitz," she said calmly. "I don't believe I heard you correctly. Surely you're not implying that you suspect President Howell of having such a lack of moral fiber."

"Of course she isn't," Zeke chimed in. "Because we all know that Barclay has so much moral fiber that he knits his underwear from the excess supply." He rubbed his knuckles against the nape of Dana's neck, and despite her best intentions she shivered just a little. His eyes narrowed and he pulled her gently in front of him and began to massage her shoulders.

The gentle touch seemed to create a war inside Dana as both warmth and chills crept through her—the heat bringing comfort and the cold creating anticipation. Very deliberately she closed her eyes and leaned back, pressing her shoulders into his palms.

She didn't realize Tiffany had come up on the stage until the blonde said brusquely, "How flattering it must be, Zeke, to still have such an electrifying impact on your wife after all these years. The way she twitches when you touch her...if I didn't know better, I'd say she doesn't like to be handled. What a pity that would be—for you."

Dana leaned back even farther against his chest and reached up to put both arms around his neck. Zeke shifted his grip, letting go of her shoulders to put his arms around her, lacing his fingers together over her tummy. He nibbled at the side of her neck and Dana jerked a little.

Tiffany's blue eyes blazed with something that looked like triumph.

Say something fast, Dana told herself. "You can always hit my ticklish spot, darling." She looked over her shoulder at him with what she hoped was an adoring smile.

What she wanted to do was swear at him. What a rotten choice of gestures, if he was trying to impress Tiffany. She'd never been able to hold still when he touched her there. How could he possibly have forgotten how sensitive that particular spot was?

Just like he's forgotten a lot of other things about you, Dana, she thought. *Very easily— because they don't matter to him anymore.*

But there was no time to think of things like that. Professor Wells had shooed the last of the students out of the auditorium, and Barclay, with his audience gone, returned to the stage.

"Hail, hail, the gang's all here," Zeke whispered into Dana's ear. His arms tightened.

"Do watch out, Zeke," Tiffany murmured. "If you're not careful, you'll squeeze that baby like a toothpaste tube."

"Baby? Who's got a baby?" Barclay said vaguely. Then his gaze locked on Tiffany. "What did you think about my announcement regarding the conference center?"

Tiffany raised her eyebrows. "You could certainly use one. Trying to hold serious events in this musty old building would be like putting a conference table in a basement closet.

Take me out for dinner and you can tell me all about your plans.''

Barclay bore her off triumphantly. Mrs. Janowitz stayed, muttering under her breath and sniffing now and then. When Zeke expressed sympathy that her allergies were bothering her and offered her a handkerchief, she put her nose in the air and stalked off.

With the sound system safely stowed, Dana was free to leave. She sank into the passenger seat of the Jaguar and said, ''I must admit I'm glad not to be walking home tonight. I'm not so sure I'd make it all the way.''

''Then it's a good thing I have a treat planned for you.''

She leaned back and closed her eyes. ''If it's dinner you have in mind, make it a drive-through.''

She actually dozed off, soothed by the purr of the engine and the leather seat that held her as secure as a cradle. When the car stopped, she opened her eyes and said, ''We're not home.''

''Next best thing,'' Zeke said cheerfully. ''Now about that faucet...''

She stared at the brightly-lit front of the home-supply store. ''You always did have a one-track mind, Zeke. It was one of the main reasons I divorced you.''

''*Tried* to divorce me. You don't have to look at faucets. You can admire porch swings instead. But if you're going to be a home-owner, Dana, you'd better learn your way around in here.''

''What happened to selling the house because it's not big enough for three?'' But she got out of the car.

She insisted on writing a check for the faucet, but she was still in shock when they got home because of the dent she'd made in her bank balance to pay for it. ''I had no idea what things like this cost.''

''You're holding that box as if there's a bar of gold inside. I told you I'd take care of it, Dana. I am living here, after all.''

''It's my house. And it's not like you don't have other obligations. I mean, you must have an apartment or something in Minneapolis.''

''That's different.''

But he didn't volunteer any details, Dana noted. Not that she'd expected him to, exactly, but she was a bit sad that he didn't feel like telling her about his life. It was a good reminder, she thought, that he was taking such an interest in the details about her out of necessity, not because he really wanted to know.

"It's only fair if I pitch in. I'm showering in your water and eating your French toast—"

The picture which sprang into her thoughts—of Zeke basking in the spray in her shower—wasn't conducive to peace of mind. So Dana said, "Speaking of food, what's for dinner?"

"Leftover pot roast." He gave her a sideways look. "At least that was the original plan."

Dana rolled her eyes. "We'll order a pizza."

The rhino was waiting on the front steps. When the car pulled in, his tail started to thump against the porch post.

"His faith in you is touching," Dana muttered.

"And with any luck, he won't like pizza and we'll be able to eat it all ourselves."

A rumble from the driveway next door announced Lou's approach as she pulled a garbage can toward the curb. "I had my son take the dog along when he went for a run," she said. "The poor thing looked like he was lonely over there, waiting for you to come home."

"I don't suppose your son would want to have a dog," Dana said hopefully.

"Of course he would." Lou's voice was cheerful. "And I'll give him permission to get one just as soon as he's self-supporting and not living in my house anymore."

"Wrong approach," Zeke said as he unlocked the door. "A successful salesperson never assumes the customer doesn't want to buy, Dana."

"It helps immensely if the product that's up for grabs has some value," Dana said dryly.

The dog grinned up at her, drooling on her shoes. He slid past her and inside the house, and Dana, tired from a long day and with her hands full with the faucet box, didn't have the stamina to try to kick him out.

In the darkened house, the blinking red light on her answering machine stood out like a beacon from the rolltop desk. Dana brightened at the thought. "Maybe his owners called." She started to count the blinks. "And called...and called again."

But though the voices on the answering machine were unfamiliar to her, Zeke obviously knew them.

"Look, Zeke," a woman's voice said. "You've got a pile of messages here. We all know how much you hate that cell phone, but would you plug the darned thing in anyway? The battery's been dead for two days now. Even you aren't that absentminded."

"My secretary," he said. "I was hoping nobody would notice. Got a piece of paper?"

"In the top drawer." Dana went on to the kitchen.

She was still standing in the doorway, the box in her hands, a few minutes later when Zeke turned off the answering machine, stuffed the sheet of paper in his pants pocket, and came up behind her. "What's the matter?" he asked.

"The faucet stopped dripping."

"That figures. As soon as you buy a new one..."

She stepped aside so he could see for himself.

She was exaggerating; the drip had not quite stopped. But in addition, a fine spray of water was now shooting out of the top of the faucet, arching a foot into the air, and falling back into the sink. At least, most of it was landing in the sink, but the tile for three feet around was damp and there was an inch-deep puddle at Dana's feet where the water had collected.

"I see the floor's not level, either," Zeke said cheerfully. "Get my bag of tools out of the car, while I look for the shutoff valve."

The dog joyously accompanied Dana all the way to the Jaguar and back, growling at shadows and nearly tripping her up a half dozen times. "Do me a favor and don't guard me so carefully, all right?" she suggested. "I'm more likely to break a leg falling over you than by being attacked by a mugger."

By the time she got back, the faucet was no longer gushing and Zeke was lying on the kitchen floor with his head and shoulders inside the cabinet under the sink. "But there's no water anywhere in the house," he warned. "I had to shut it off at the main valve."

"Then I'll order sodas with the pizza instead of making coffee."

"You really know how to hurt a guy." His voice echoed a little.

Dana phoned in the pizza order and pulled up a tall stool so she could perch on it. "Do you need to return any of those calls before you start on the faucet?''

''They can wait till the cell phone's charged up again.''

''Did you honestly let it die on purpose? Why?''

''Because I'm tired of being tied to it. It's too easy to call me, so everybody does.''

''It's not just the phone, though, is it, Zeke?'' she said quietly.

He pushed himself out from under the sink. ''Very perceptive of you.''

''You hate your business.''

''I hate being in business. There's a difference.''

''It all boils down to wanting to be on the beach instead,'' Dana mused. ''There's one thing I don't understand, though. Why do you insist on selling the company to Tiffany?''

''The money, darling.'' His voice was crisp.

''But why Tiffany? Why can't you sell it to someone else? Unless she's the only one who wants it.''

''No, there are others who are interested. But she's the only one who's able and willing to pay top dollar.''

"Money isn't everything, Zeke. I don't feel as if I know you anymore. You never used to be so obsessed with money."

He was working the old faucet loose. "Are you certain about what I used to be like? As you've pointed out yourself, we never had any money to obsess about."

"People don't change that much," Dane mused. "If you'd been the money-hungry type, you wouldn't have paid the attorney for our divorce. You'd have intentionally stuck me with the bill."

"You believed me when I said I paid it? Of course, it was a nice story."

Why is he trying to pick a fight? To stop me from asking questions...but which questions?

"Anyway, it doesn't take a whole lot of money if your big goal is to lie on a beach for the rest of your life."

Zeke opened his mouth, and for an instant she thought he was going to tell the truth. Then he smiled wryly and said, "The rest of my life could be a long time, sweetheart. Swim trunks, beach towels, suntan lotion...it runs into big bucks."

"All right, have it your way," she mused. "You're not going to tell me, so I'll figure it out for myself. You definitely want every last penny you can squeeze out of Tiffany. But why? If you were promoting a cause of some sort, I think you'd go to work for it, not just provide funds. And you're not trying to build a monument to your ego—if Barclay offered to name the new conference center after you because of a seven-and-a-half-million-dollar contribution, you'd tear up the check.''

He opened the box containing the new faucet and ostentatiously spread the instruction sheet out beside the sink. But Dana knew he was still listening to her, because she'd never seen him read the instructions on how to do anything.

''I know you don't have any family,'' she went on, ''so there's no sweet gray-haired aunt to be kept in a retirement home, and no sister in a wheelchair suffering from a wasting disease.''

For a moment she thought he wasn't going to answer at all. When he finally did, his voice was deeper than usual. ''Go on, Dana. I can't wait to hear what you come up with next.''

Family.... When she'd said family, he'd flinched. She'd seen the muscles in his back and shoulders go tight for just an instant. *Family...*

She decided to probe a little harder. ''You're not trying to make a fortune for my sake, obviously, but I'm the only thing close to a family that you've got.''

He looked sideways at her. ''Sure of that, are you? Maybe I have a bunch of kids I haven't told you about.''

She dismissed the possibility without a second thought. ''If you had, you'd have used them as an excuse to get rid of Tiffany, instead of bothering with me. It would have worked, too—she wouldn't take on any man who refused to put her first in his life. That's one of the reasons she wants you to work for her instead of staying with your own business—so your obligations to your employees won't get in her way, either.'' She snapped her fingers. ''Got it. *Employees.*''

He was looking at her with admiration. ''You are one downright decent little plotter, Dana. Next time I want a conspiracy arranged, I'll definitely bring you into it. Heck, I'll put you in charge.''

''Even though you're selling the business, you want to look after your employees. It's not an enormous company—what did you say? A couple of hundred employees?—and so you're all sort of family. How many secretaries scold their bosses like yours does? So by selling to Tiffany...'' She frowned. ''The trouble is, I can't see her as all that wonderful an employer.''

''She's all right, if kept at a distance. And they'll have a choice about whether or not they work for her.''

The final piece dropped into place in Dana's mind. ''She's offering so much money that they can all retire?''

''You just don't quit, do you? No, they aren't all going to be able to retire, but they'll each get a nice chunk of change. Some of my employees have been with me from the beginning. There are a dozen who worked the first couple of years without regular paychecks. They're more like partners and they deserve a reward.''

''So that's why you want every dime you can get,'' Dana said slowly. ''Not for yourself, but for them.''

''I'm not a saint, Dana. I'm not going to turn down my share.''

"But your employees will get most of it. Right?"

"It'll be split up according to the time each employee has been with the company, and not every one will get enough money that they'll never have to work again. But they'll be able to retire early, or start a business of their own, or stay home for a few years to raise their kids."

She stared at him for a long moment, and warmth began to bubble up from deep inside her. "No wonder you weren't very sympathetic with Ned Marsh for wanting to cash in without having done any of the work. What about the beach?"

"You're the one who suggested that was what I wanted," he pointed out.

"So what do you really want, Zeke?"

He sighed. "I want what I used to have, back when I was tinkering with switches—before I got successful. It was fun to play with ideas, try to create something new and make it work. Then suddenly I had a hot invention, and a patent attorney, and some employees, and a factory, and then more employees, and a balance sheet—"

"And a cell phone?"

He nodded. "And never any time to think about anything else. I'm much better at figuring out ideas than I am at making numbers add up—but the last few years there have been a lot more numbers than ideas."

"You want to be independent again."

"Without anybody to answer to or be responsible for. So it seemed to me that it was worth a little personal sacrifice to make a deal with Tiffany, in order to take care of my people. But it wasn't worth sacrificing my independence altogether. Tiffany's concept of research and development is to create an infinite number of dinky improvements to the original switch, while my thinking runs more along the lines of something completely new." He set the faucet handle in place and started to cinch it tight.

"Which means you have something in mind already."

"Only a possibility. Until I have some time, I have no idea if it'll work."

"I'm impressed," she said. "You're quite a guy, Zeke. But then I've always known that."

He turned to look at her, and Dana's breath caught in her throat. What had made her say that? And what was he thinking? His eyes had gone very dark. Surely he didn't think she was offering some kind of invitation—

She said hastily, "About the conference center...you don't have to give me the seven and a half million dollars. I mean, now that I know why you really want all that money—"

"You haven't earned it yet," Zeke said coolly.

She released a long breath of relief. They were back on solid ground, and next time she'd be more careful. "I know. We're no farther along now than when we started. The way Tiffany looked at us this afternoon—"

"Can you blame her? You jump a foot whenever I touch you."

"Well, if you'd leave my ticklish spots alone and stop startling me—"

"We need to do some serious work, you know." He tried the faucet handle, which turned smoothly.

"And exactly what do you mean by that?" Dana asked warily.

"Practice, my dear. Practice." He put the screwdriver down and wiped his hands on a towel. "Take, for instance, the basic hug. There are a number of ways to do it. The sideways hug..." He put an arm around her shoulders. "The A-frame hug, leaning toward each other and using both arms but leaving a mile of space between the bodies." He demonstrated. "Or the full bear hug..." He drew her close, molding her close against him from shoulder to knee. "Also known as the lover's hug."

Dana's breathing had gone shallow and fast. But then there wasn't room in her lungs for a full breath, because he was holding her so closely.

"That's better," he whispered against her lips. "You didn't even flinch that time."

The softness of his mouth against hers seemed to be contagious, for every muscle in her body suddenly felt like jelly.

"You haven't forgotten, any more than I have." He kissed her, very gently, as if he knew that exerting more than the slightest pressure would cause her to collapse entirely. He nibbled at her lips as if she were a new kind of candy, one he would have only a single opportunity to enjoy. One he intended to make last as long as was humanly possible.

She wanted more. She tried to say so but her vocal cords didn't seem to work anymore. At any rate, he seemed to understand, because his next kiss was hungry, demanding—just the way Dana felt.

Her ears were ringing from lack of oxygen. No…it wasn't her ears, that was the doorbell.

"It's the pizza," Zeke said.

She wanted to tell him that the last thing on earth she wanted just now was pizza. But her sense of self-preservation, dimmed though it was by the assault on her senses, stopped her.

"I'll get the door." Her voice felt rusty, and she had to hang on to the edge of the kitchen counter till her head stopped spinning.

The bell pealed again as she dug in her handbag. But she couldn't find enough cash to pay for the pizza—and after the spree at the home-supply store she didn't dare write another check. So she went back to the kitchen.

Zeke was whistling under his breath as he checked all the connections between pipes and faucet. He looked up as she came in. "No pizza?"

"No money," she said just as succinctly.

He reached for his wallet. "It's bad enough that you're blackmailing me for millions, but now you won't even buy me a pizza when I've knocked myself out to fix your plumbing. You ungrateful wench."

His voice was low and rich and full of idle good humor. It sounded like warm honey, Dana thought. She watched as he pulled a bill from his wallet, brushed it against his lips as if kissing it goodbye, and held it out to her.

That was when she knew that marrying him hadn't been the biggest mistake of her life after all. And neither had divorcing him.

The biggest mistake of her life was that she hadn't learned anything from the whole experience, and so when he'd reappeared she'd done it all over again. She'd thought she was immune because of the hurt she'd suffered, so she had underestimated the effect that his charm, his attraction, his sheer sexy skill could have on her.

And she'd fallen for him harder than ever.

She had to escape, had to get away before he saw the shock—or worse, the knowledge— mirrored in her face. She plucked the money out of his hand and turned away.

The trouble was, she reminded herself, that nothing had changed. He'd always been able to kiss her senseless, always been able to make her laugh and forget their quarrels—for a while. That hadn't been enough to make a marriage work six years ago, and it wasn't enough now.

But even knowing the truth was no armor against the feelings. No protection against desire. No defense against the hunger that filled her.

She'd been within an inch, there in the kitchen, of begging him to forget about the faucet and take her to bed. Half of her still wished she had, but the other half knew that it wouldn't have been enough. She wanted to make love with him, yes, but she wanted—needed—more than that.

She wanted him to love her, as she loved him. She wanted the pretense they were living to be real.

But wanting wasn't enough. Zeke had said it himself... *It was worth a little personal sacrifice to make a deal with Tiffany.*

"And I," Dana said under her breath, "am the little personal sacrifice he's making."

The bell rang yet again. "I'm coming," she said irritably and pulled open the door. "How much?"

Then she realized that there was no pizza delivery person. A couple faced her instead. Their hair was touched with light from the yellowed old porch lamp above their heads—a harsh light, Dana realized, which must show her as slack-jawed and speechless.

Barclay and Tiffany were standing on the front porch. ''Do pardon us for barging in,'' Tiffany said, and before Dana could stop her she was across the threshold and inside.

CHAPTER NINE

DANA, still half stunned by the discovery she'd just made about her own idiocy, was in no condition to hold Tiffany at bay. She stood frozen as Tiffany's gaze swept the room. The blonde looked triumphant as she purred, "I stopped to see Zeke. But he doesn't seem to be here. I don't suppose you can tell me where he is?"

It was an interesting way to phrase the question, Dana thought. In fact, it hadn't really been a question at all. Of course Tiffany wouldn't simply ask, *Where is he?* She'd added the implication that Dana couldn't possibly know.

The dog crept behind Dana and leaned against her calves, almost knocking her down. She might have given him a push so she could stand up straight again, but she could feel him trembling. *Poor Rhino,* she thought. He seemed to be every bit as attuned to the tension in the room as Dana was.

"And don't tell me Zeke's indisposed, or in the bedroom waiting for you," Tiffany added briskly. "Because you're the one who's supposed to be sick, and that excuse is only good once. Besides, any woman who had Zeke Ferris in her bedroom wouldn't be answering the door."

True, Dana thought. *Crude, but absolutely true.*

How could she have missed seeing what was happening to her? How could she have dismissed the feelings Zeke inspired in her as the mere vestiges of long-ago-dimmed passions?

But right now wasn't the time to be thinking about it, she told herself. Not with Tiffany standing there, waiting for an answer and poised to follow it with an attack.

Zeke called, "Dana, come here! Now!"

He couldn't have timed it better if he'd tried. Dana would have suspected him of eavesdropping, except she knew if he'd had any idea who was in the living room, he'd have asked politely instead of issuing a command.

Tiffany looked disappointed.

"You were half right," Dana said sweetly. "Only he's waiting for me in the kitchen, not the bedroom. It's one of those little homeowner-type projects, so I'm afraid we're a bit too busy to entertain just now. If you'll excuse me…?''

"Dammit, Dana," Zeke bellowed, "get in here. I need a hand!''

Dana swiftly considered her options. The last thing she wanted to do was to invite Tiffany and Barclay inside. Of course, Tiffany was already in—and she appeared to have taken root in the floor. Judging by the blatant curiosity in her face, dislodging her was likely to be neither fast nor easy.

Dana could stand there and argue, but short of actually shoving her out the door, she was probably not going to get rid of the blonde anytime soon. In the meantime, Zeke—not knowing what was going on—might keep on yelling. And if he happened to say anything about blackmail, or deals…

"I'll be right back," she said hastily to Tiffany, and raised her voice. "Coming, darling!''

Silence fell in the kitchen. One thing about Zeke, she thought, he wasn't slow on the uptake.

But from the kitchen doorway she could see that he hadn't necessarily gone silent because he'd gotten the message, but because he had his hands full. He'd obviously turned the water supply back on, because the faucet was spraying like an out-of-control fire hose. Every seam and connection appeared to be leaking. Some were merely dripping, some were oozing, but a couple were under high pressure—one was shooting water sideways straight into his chest with a hiss that sounded as if it was about to boil. And, she saw, water was cascading out of the open cabinet under the sink as if there were other leaks she couldn't even see.

Zeke was leaning over the faucet, trying to control the spray with towels and rags, but he was obviously having minimal success. His shirt was soaked and even his eyebrows were dripping.

"It looks like you fixed the faucet, all right." Dana was surprised by the calmness of her own voice. "Fixed it but good. We have company, by the way."

"Unless it's a plumber, I don't care. Turn the main valve off again."

"But I don't know where it is."

"Some homeowner you are. Grab this, then, and hold on tight while I get the valve."

Dana made a face, but she gamely seized another handful of towels and tried to stop the spray. "At least it's not scalding hot," she muttered. "Though a cold shower isn't exactly what I had in mind."

The dog had followed her in. He looked up at her inquisitively and then started to lap up water from the floor.

"Maybe you're good for something after all," Dana told him.

By the time Zeke returned, the front of her suit was drenched and her hair was hanging limply in her eyes. And the faucet was still spraying.

"I thought you were going to turn off the valve," she gasped.

"I did, but there's still water in the system. It'll stop soon."

The spray weakened as he spoke, and the hiss died away. Dana carefully unwound the wet towels to take a look. "What happened, anyway?"

"One of the connections was still loose, and when I tried to tighten it, the supply pipe twisted and split. The plumbing under that sink must be fifty years old. I don't suppose, when you bought the house, that you thought about having somebody take a look at this kind of thing?"

"No," Dana admitted.

"Too bad. If you'd hired an inspector, you could sue him for not warning you."

Tiffany's brittle laugh split the air, giving Dana the first warning that the woman hadn't stayed in the living room as she'd been asked to do. She glanced over her shoulder to see that both Tiffany and Barclay had followed her into the kitchen. "So nice of you to offer your help," she said under her breath.

"When *she* bought the house?" Tiffany asked. "Goodness, Zeke, that sounds as if you didn't have a say in the choice. How very interesting."

Dana ignored her. Pushing her hair out of her eyes, she looked straight at Zeke. "But we can't do without water. You can fix it, right?"

"Not till at least tomorrow. That whole section of pipe is shot."

"I think, myself," Tiffany mused, "that it's a good thing Zeke chose electricity to tinker with instead of plumbing—or he might still be fiddling unsuccessfully in his garage instead of being an outstanding young entrepreneur."

The doorbell rang again. *Now what?* Dana thought warily, and even the dog whined in anticipation.

But it was only the forgotten pizza delivery. Dana retrieved the money Zeke had given her from the kitchen counter where she'd dropped it when she'd taken over faucet duty, tried futilely to pat it dry, handed it over to the deliveryman, and carried the pizza box into the kitchen.

"Sorry we can't offer you a cup of tea or something," she told Barclay and Tiffany, "but without water this isn't exactly on the same level as Baron's Hill."

Barclay spoke up for the first time. "Baron's Hill. That's the answer. You can come and stay at Baron's Hill."

Dana felt a little light-headed at the idea. "That's very generous of you, Barclay, but we can go to a hotel or something. We'll figure it out."

"That's the thing," Barclay said. "You can't go to a hotel, not in this town. Tiffany was telling me over dinner how crowded all the hotels are this weekend. There's some convention going on that has everything full."

Dana happened to glance at Tiffany in time to see the woman's face tighten. For an instant, there was nothing in the least attractive about her. She looked as hard as stone and just about as cuddly.

But within seconds Tiffany had regained her self-control and was smiling once more. "What a shame that I didn't ask for a two-bedroom suite when I checked in. You could come and have a pajama party with me."

My fondest dream, Dana thought. *A midnight heart-to-heart with Tiffany Rowe.*

She sent a hard look at Zeke, who only shrugged.

"That's very kind of you, Barclay," she said, "but—"

"I insist," he said grandly. "With everything you do for the university, Dana, this is the least we can do for you in return. Go pack a bag and plan to stay for the weekend—you'll need to be there tomorrow anyway to oversee the dinner party plans."

One sure thing about Barclay, Dana thought. *He's always pragmatic when his own interests are at stake.* "That's true," she admitted.

"Then it's settled," Barclay said. "I'll drop Tiffany at her hotel and meet you at Baron's Hill."

Tiffany pursed her lips. "Barclay, dear, I'm sure you didn't mean it to sound as if you're in a hurry to be rid of me."

That was careless of you, Barclay, Dana thought.

He began to stammer.

"You don't have to change your plans, Barclay," Dana said. "I have a key, remember?" *And I'd rather not sit around the drawing room at Baron's Hill making conversation tonight anyway.*

Barclay was obviously grateful for the straw she offered. "Yes, of course you can do that, Dana. All the guest rooms are kept ready—I insist that the housekeepers have them prepared at all times. So you can use any of them."

Tiffany's eyes narrowed. "How interesting," she purred. "Your very own key?"

"I've never actually used it," Dana said. "The housekeeping staff or the caterers have always been there to let me in."

"Oh, that's right," Tiffany murmured. "You've been spending so much time in charge at Baron's Hill that you must feel right at home there. Well, we'll leave you to enjoy your pizza." She linked her arm into

Barclay's. "Shall we try out that new night-club you were telling me about?"

Dana ushered them to the door. Barclay hung back a bit. "Thanks, Dana," he whispered. "I'd hate for her to have gotten the wrong idea about why you've got that key. Isn't she wonderful?"

Wonderful? *In a manner of speaking,* Dana thought. *Tiffany was certainly a wonder.*

"So lucky, really, that Zeke came along when he did," Barclay went on.

Because otherwise, he was obviously thinking, he'd have been stuck with Dana and couldn't have taken up with Tiffany. *Dana, my girl, you've just been dumped.*

She closed the door and went back to the kitchen where Zeke was still mopping up the mess. "I thought you told me Tiffany was subtle. Personally, I think she's about as subtle as a ballistic missile."

Zeke shrugged. "Finding out about you has upset her. She's on the defensive, so of course she's not being quite as smooth as normal."

He might be right about that, Dana thought, because all in all, they'd escaped relatively unscathed. Tiffany hadn't even insisted on sticking around to spy on them as they packed.

So why did Dana feel as if she was still trying to dodge a bullet?

Baron's Hill was quiet and almost entirely dark, except for the security lights which were always on. Dana had walked through the entire mansion before, but never so late at night, and never alone. The house seemed huge after her own small cottage, even larger than it did in daylight, and their footsteps seemed to echo.

She stopped at the top of the long staircase and opened the first door. "This is the main guest suite. There's a bedroom, of course, but also a sitting room—and there's a couch that folds out into a bed." Dana snapped on a light and surveyed the antiques which filled the sitting room.

Zeke looked around with much less interest. "All very nice, but I don't think we should use it."

"The suite?"

"No, the fold-out bed. I wouldn't put it past Tiffany to talk Barclay into surprising us by barging in tomorrow morning with coffee and croissants."

"You actually think she'd ask him to spy on whether we shared a bed? Get real, Zeke."

"You don't think she'd do it?"

"Of course she'd ask him. But Barclay wouldn't do anything as common as carry a breakfast tray—that's a job for the housekeeping staff."

Zeke dropped her overnight bag next to a velvet-covered fainting couch. "That's what I thought." He lay down on the couch, ankles crossed and arms folded behind his head, looking utterly at ease.

Dana stood at the foot of the couch, hands on hips, and surveyed him. "What do you mean? If you knew Barclay wouldn't do anything he considers servants' work, why would you think—"

"That's not what I was talking about. You've never been serious about Barclay, have you? You just confirmed it."

Dana felt as if she'd swallowed her tongue. She'd been so cautious to watch every word and action that might tell Zeke what a fool she'd made of herself by falling in love with him all over again that she'd completely forgotten to consider what she said about Barclay.

Too late now, she thought. *No sense in denying it.*

"You did seem to enjoy the idea," she said. "And it hardly seemed sporting to disillusion you when you were having so much fun nick-naming my kids and everything."

"I could have a lot more fun doing other things."

Other things. No need to ask what he had in mind. There was a rough edge to his voice that made Dana shiver in anticipation.

Anticipation? she thought, stunned. Surely she had more sense than that. Yes, she felt an enormously strong physical attraction for the man. Not only was he sexy as sin, but her own memories were enough to make her skin steam. And not just memories from six years ago, from the days when she had thought that loving him was enough to make their marriage succeed. Those memories had faded just enough that she could convince herself she was remembering an ideal, not the reality.

The memory that was really giving her problems was the one from just this morning, because it was so painfully fresh. Waking up in his arms had startled her so badly that she had regained her senses only with difficulty. And then she'd wished that she hadn't stopped to think, that she'd just let herself feel…and act on her feelings.

Nonsense, she told herself. The most idiotic thing she could have done was to make love with him. There was absolutely no doubt about it. Nothing which had happened since had changed that.

So why was she even thinking about it?

She'd thought making conversation with Barclay in the drawing room would be tough, Dana thought. How foolish of her—because that would have been nothing like as difficult as small talk with Zeke in the guest suite.

''We really need to add a bookshelf to each guest room,'' she muttered. Why hadn't it occurred to her to bring a magazine, at least?

''Maybe the guests haven't missed books because they have other forms of entertainment.''

Dana could feel herself turning pink, but fortunately Zeke wasn't looking. He'd pushed himself up from the fainting couch and strolled over to the bedroom door.

''I don't suppose there's a room with a larger bed,'' he mused.

"I've never actually measured them. Why?"

"It probably doesn't matter anyway. No matter how big, if we're sharing it, it's likely to mean trouble."

Dana was stung. "If you think because of what happened this morning that I can't keep my hands off you—"

"Oh, I suppose you can. But the question is, do you want to, Dana? Really, honestly want to?"

"Of course I—" She swallowed hard.

One mistake was enough for a whole lifetime, she reminded herself. And she'd made hers, on a grand scale. It would be insane to repeat it.

And yet...

She remembered thinking, just a day or two ago, that if they hadn't made the mistake of getting married, they might still be friends. But the fact was they had been married, they had been lovers—and now there was no going back.

Even if it were possible for her to forget everything they had shared, Dana wouldn't be satisfied now with his friendship, because she wanted so much more than that. She couldn't be an ordinary friend—the kind whom a man called up because he wanted advice on the current woman in his life.

Not when she wanted to *be* the woman in his life.

You can't make that happen, Dana, she told herself. *You can't force him to want you just because you want him.*

At least, she couldn't demand that he feel the same way she did. But in fact, he did want her. She could see it in his eyes, in the tension of his body as he stood in the bedroom door looking at her.

She couldn't have everything she wanted. But she certainly wanted whatever she could have.

He had asked her to give him three months—ninety days of pretending once more to be his wife. Now that she had met Tiffany, Dana thought perhaps he had been unduly optimistic. Or perhaps that was only wishful thinking on her part, to hope that Tiffany would require even more convincing—and even more time—than Zeke had counted on.

In any case, the length of time was beside the point. For a while—whether it ended up being a few weeks or a few months—Dana could once more be the woman in his life. She couldn't ever be his wife again, and she suspected no woman ever would be—Zeke had made it clear that marriage had not been to his taste.

But for a while she could be his companion. She could be his friend. She could be his lover.

Seven and a half million dollars couldn't buy him a ticket into her bedroom, she had told him on that first night. And it was true—but in fact he didn't need to offer her anything but himself.

She would have to be very careful. Careful not to forget that this was temporary. Careful not to let slip that she wasn't simply playing the game as he had asked. Careful not to show, when it was all over, that she was anything but relieved.

There would be fallout, she was sure of that. But she would deal with it later. She would have a lifetime to sort it out. Now she had only a few weeks—if she was very lucky, a few months—to store up enough memories to last her for a lifetime.

This time, she knew better than to think in terms of forever. So this time, she would not let a moment pass without savoring it and creating a memory to keep her warm when he was once more gone.

Zeke seemed to see her decision in her face. But he didn't appear to relax, as she'd half expected he would. If anything the tension in his body seemed to increase.

He took a step toward her, and she met him halfway across the sitting room. Suddenly shy, she laid both hands against his chest, and when she felt the pounding of his heart she knew that she'd made the right choice. *Seize the moment,* she told herself, and twined her arms around his neck to pull him down to her.

His kiss was tentative, reminiscent of the first time—all those years ago. Impatient for more, Dana pressed herself against him.

''You'd better be sure of what you want,'' Zeke warned. His voice was raspy. ''Another minute and there won't be any backing out.''

''Because I've already used my get-out-of-jail-free card,'' she agreed. ''So I guess that means if you have a set of handcuffs lying around, you'd better use them.''

He kissed her instead. Really kissed her—and under that gentle assault Dana couldn't have been more helpless even if he'd tied her up with ropes and chains. Breathless and aching and unable to stand up on her own, she clung to him until he picked her up and carried her into the bedroom.

And though she tried to remember the rules she had set up for herself, after a while her mind stopped working altogether, leaving only hunger and the instinct to satisfy it—and the desire to please him as much as he was pleasing her.

Dana had no idea what time they finally drifted off to sleep. She only knew that she was blissfully exhausted and so relaxed that she felt as if every bone in her body had been replaced with a chunk of chewing gum.

So exhausted and relaxed was she, in fact, that even the murmur of voices in the hallway outside the bedroom didn't rouse her, as it probably would have in any hotel. Even when the bedroom door burst open and the chandelier overhead flared like the sudden explosion of a warhead, she was slow to react. She sat up and raised a hand to shield her eyes from the glare, staring through the sudden brilliance to the doorway, unable to comprehend what she saw.

It was Zeke who pulled the sheet up to cover her. He had obviously taken in at a glance what Dana saw as if in slow motion.

Tiffany, standing in the doorway with one hand on the light switch and the other clutching the handle of a suitcase. Tiffany, with her jaw almost touching her chest. Tiffany, blinking and saying, in not quite her usual smooth voice, "My goodness, I had no idea you were using this room. Barclay invited me to come and stay, too, so we can have a house party."

She backed out of the room, leaving the light on.

"I wonder how many rooms she looked into before she found us," Zeke muttered. "Well, you were right about the coffee and croissants. No need to worry about Barclay barging in, since Tiffany took care of it herself."

"I guess that's that," Dana said, trying to keep her voice even. But now what? Now that Tiffany knew, absolutely for certain, that they were not just putting on a show...

Dana tried to ignore the gnawing ache in the pit of her stomach—the ache that said her life had just fallen apart all over again.

* * *

No question about it, Zeke thought. This time, Tiffany had gotten the message loud and clear. She could hardly ignore the evidence of her own eyes; seeing the two of them tangled together like that could leave no doubt whatsoever about what they'd been doing.

His eyelids felt grainy inside. He glanced at the clock as he crossed the room to turn off the chandelier Tiffany had left burning.

Three o'clock in the morning? That must have been some nightclub.

Or, more likely, it had taken all of Tiffany's wiles to keep Barclay away from Baron's Hill so late into the night and then to talk him into inviting her home with him so she could burst in on them when they would be most vulnerable. No doubt she'd hoped—expected—to find them grimly waiting out the night. Playing cards maybe, or lying side by side, fully dressed and with a barricade down the center of the bed.

There was a time when he'd have given half the value of his business to see that look of utter astonishment in her eyes. He just wished it hadn't been tonight....

What are you, nuts? This outcome was exactly what he'd wanted—a nice clean end to the problem. After tonight, Tiffany would have to see reason about the employment contract. She would have to come to terms regarding the sale. And once that agreement was completed...

It would all be over.

Frowning, he climbed back into bed. But something was different. Suddenly there was an empty space in the warm center of the bed, and Dana was lying with her back to him, her pillow cradled in her arms.

That's enough of that, he thought, and leaned over her to run a gentle finger down her spine. "Since we're awake..." he whispered.

She didn't move, didn't even flinch at the touch of his lips against the ticklish spot on her neck. Her voice came out of the darkness, cool and level. "Surely it isn't necessary to put on any more of a show. She won't be back."

A glass of ice water to the face couldn't have chilled him more. *Putting on a show...* What the hell was she talking about? She couldn't mean that she'd expected Tiffany to do something of the sort, so she'd set about making sure that the picture Tiffany saw would convince her. Could she?

You're the one who said you wouldn't be surprised if someone came bursting in, he reminded himself. *Dana just took your logic a step further.*

Pain began to grind in his gut.

And then he remembered something else. Tiffany had been stunned when she turned on the lights and saw them, but there had been another expression in her eyes when she backed away. It was an expression he'd seen before.

In the space of half a minute, Tiffany's surprise had turned to cold-blooded calculation.

Damn, he thought. The woman was beginning to seriously get on his nerves.

Dana didn't expect to sleep. In fact, she didn't think she had slept—but when she opened her eyes sunlight was streaming in the window and Zeke was no longer in the room, much less in the bed. She hadn't heard him go, and he hadn't left a note.

But there was no surprise about that, she thought drearily.

It was already midmorning when Dana came downstairs, and the housekeepers were bustling to get ready for the evening's dinner party. Curiosity rolled like a wave through the staff when she appeared. Dana didn't blame them; Barclay wasn't the sort to hold impromptu house parties, or invite overnight guests on the spur of the moment. For him to have three visitors on a single night...

She poured herself a cup of coffee and took her notebook into the music room—the housekeepers were already working everywhere else—intending to sit where it was quiet to make her list of tasks for the day. She was getting a very late start, and she'd need all the organizational power she could muster.

It was probably just as well, she thought, that she was going to be busy all day. She wouldn't know what to say to Zeke anyway—and obviously he didn't have much to say to her, either.

She hesitated at the door, recalling that the last time she'd been in the music room was when Barclay had proposed. *And I thought that was major trouble.*

Tiffany was standing by the bow window which overlooked the garden at the side of the house, with one slim hand raised to hold back the lace curtain.

Pensive pose number three, Dana thought. "Good morning, Tiffany."

Tiffany turned slowly from the window, surveyed Dana over from head to foot, and then looked past her to the hallway. "You must have worn Zeke out last night, if he's still in bed."

"Perhaps I energized him instead," Dana said coolly. "He's already left."

"In that case, tell him—whenever you see him next—that I'll be expecting to hear from him." Tiffany let the curtain fall back into place and picked up her suitcase. "I presume someone can call a cab for me?"

From the doorway a deep voice said, "Certainly, madam."

Dana spun around to face a tall, gaunt-faced man in a black suit. "Mr. Beeler—you're back. Nobody told me."

"I only decided this morning that I was up to the job," he said. "I will summon a taxi, and then if you'll fill me in on the plans you've already made for this evening's dinner, Ms. Mulholland, I'll take over."

I'm free, Dana thought. Her heart lifted for a moment, and then dropped like a rock as she remembered how very, very free she was.

*   *   *

The Jaguar was parked in the driveway beside her house. Dana stopped dead when she saw it, wondering for an instant if she'd conjured it up from her own wishes. But it was indisputably there, and so was Zeke, for she heard his voice as she opened the door.

"I'll call you as soon as I get in, then," he said, and she heard the snap of a cell phone closing.

As soon as I get in… He was leaving. But that was no surprise. Obviously she didn't need to deliver Tiffany's message after all.

He was on the floor, half under the sink, when she came into the kitchen. The dog gave a single, sharp bark.

"That's great," Dana said wryly. "Defend my house against me, there's a good guard dog."

Zeke pushed himself out from under the sink. "I didn't expect you home anytime soon."

"Sorry to disappoint you. The man who regularly manages Baron's Hill is back on the job."

"So you're out of one."

"Just back to the regular routine. I see you followed your secretary's orders and recharged the cell phone."

"Yeah. She was starting to get a little shrill about it." He reached under the sink. "Sorry I couldn't leave the car for you but I needed to get supplies if you're going to have water."

Not *we*, Dana noted. *You.*

"You couldn't leave me a note?" She knew she sounded bitter, and she didn't care. "Oh, right—you never could manage to do that."

"I assumed you could figure out where I'd be. And I also thought that the less evidence I left lying around Baron's Hill, the better."

"In case Tiffany popped in again? By the way, she wants you to call her. Unless you were talking to her just now, of course."

"No. It wasn't her." He gave a final turn to the faucet connections. "That should do it. Do you want to turn on the water or shall I?"

"Oh, you should definitely have the honor."

She heard the creak of the shutoff valve opening, and turned the handle of the faucet. A puff of air shot out, then a burst of water, then more air—as if the pipes were hiccuping. But there were no leaks and no drips.

"All that air will work its way out of the system," Zeke said. "It'll take a little time."

Dana nodded. She squirted dishwashing soap into the water and began shifting dishes from the drain board to the sink.

"Dana," he said quietly. "I have to go back to Minneapolis."

She didn't trust herself to turn around. "It's been fun, Zeke. Let me know how it all turns out."

He didn't slam the front door. He didn't even let it bang behind him. But she heard the soft, oddly final click of the latch, even over the sound of running water.

He wasn't angry, she thought. He was relieved. He had accomplished what he'd set out to do.

Only then did she see that he'd left a set of keys—the set he'd had the hardware store make for him on the day he'd fixed the gutter—on the drain board. It was the final straw, forcing her to admit that he wasn't coming back.

Dana bit her lip hard, but even that didn't keep tears from falling into the dishwater.

CHAPTER TEN

AUTUMN was almost gone, and now when Dana walked to work she bundled up in a long wool coat and wrapped a scarf around her throat. As for exercising the dog, she was considering taking up jogging—at least the activity would keep her warmer, and Rhino made no secret of his preference for speed.

"I realize that in your opinion I come in a poor second to Zeke," she told the dog late one afternoon as he tugged impatiently on his leash. "But I'm the only thing you've got. Get used to it."

He licked her hand apologetically and rubbed the top of his head against her wrist.

Dana smiled a little. "Don't get a big head over it," she told him, "but I'm kind of glad that nobody ever claimed you."

The day had been milder than the last few, and they'd walked farther than usual—into a neighborhood Dana hadn't visited in years. It was only when she looked up at the vaguely familiar outline of a big old foursquare house that she realized where she was. She'd crossed the street which used to separate the campus from the worst neighborhood anywhere around, and she was standing in front of the Quagmire.

The house hadn't been reduced to rubble by Zeke and his multitude of roommates after all. In fact, all things considered, it was looking pretty good. Sometime in the last six years it had obviously fallen into more careful hands, and now the exterior sported a fresh coat of white paint, the sagging front steps and missing shutters had been replaced, and there were curtains at the windows instead of the sheets and beach towels the guys had tacked up at random. The lawn was neatly trimmed and a child's tricycle stood on the sidewalk in front.

Funny, she thought. If she'd had to bet, all those years ago, on which would survive—her marriage or the Quagmire—she'd have staked her life on the marriage. But the house had not only survived, it had obviously prospered. While Dana and Zeke...

It had been three weeks since he'd gone back to Minneapolis, and she hadn't heard a word. Not that she'd expected to, exactly— though she had thought that he'd be in touch as soon as it was safe to start the divorce in motion again. But perhaps it was time to stop waiting and hire an attorney. Get all of this behind her.

Not that it would ever go away, she knew. It had taken three weeks just for the constant, stabbing pain to settle into a heavy, dull ache. She expected she'd always have that, but at least it was bearable most of the time. Some nights she could even sleep.

She glanced at her watch and despite Rhino's objections, she turned toward home. Tonight was Barclay's regular cocktail party for donors, faculty, and staff, and this time Dana was an invited guest, not the one in charge.

How much difference a month makes. Just four weeks ago today her biggest concern had been getting the afternoon tea guests out of the way in time for the start of the cocktail party. Then Barclay had dropped that bombshell of a proposal on her, and Zeke had reappeared and cut an even wider swathe through her life than he had the first time.

She'd debated turning down the invitation, but in the end she'd decided that the faster she got back into the regular rhythms of life, the better. And the regular rhythms of her life included things like visiting Baron's Hill—which she hadn't done since she and Zeke had spent the night in the guest suite. Sooner or later, though, she would have to go back to the mansion. She might as well get it over with.

But she deliberately waited till the party would be well under way, when Barclay would be occupied and her own entrance was less likely to be noted. Mr. Beeler, looking considerably less cadaverous now that he was fully recovered from his pneumonia, greeted her at the door, hung her coat in the guest closet, and bowed her into the drawing room.

She'd delayed so long that even the faculty guests had all arrived. Professor Wells was already standing beside the fireplace with a Scotch and water in her hand, talking to a particularly earnest-looking alumnus. She waved her glass, and Dana—interpreting the gesture as a plea for rescue—went to get a sparkling water before joining her.

Barclay was standing at the portable bar. It was the first time she'd come face-to-face with him since the night he'd left her house with Tiffany in tow—the night of the ill-fated house party. "Hello, Dana." He looked on beyond her. "You're alone? Well, I'm sure Zeke has plenty to keep him busy these days. I understand he's sold his business."

I'd be the last to know. Dana tried for a mysterious smile. "Where did you hear that news?"

"I read it sometime in the last few days. In the *Wall Street Journal,* I believe."

Then it was no doubt true, Dana thought. And now that things were finalized, she'd be hearing from Zeke soon—unless she heard from his attorney instead. If he went ahead and filed for the divorce himself...

"So is he going to come through with that donation you were talking about?" Barclay asked.

She had almost forgotten telling Barclay that tall tale, so she hadn't thought of a way to let him down easily. But she'd better find one fast, Dana told herself, because the odds of Zeke delivering on the deal they'd made were about the same as the chances of the quadrangle being hit by a sandstorm before the night was out.

She'd told Zeke herself that she wouldn't hold him to the bargain they'd made. It had been one thing to shake him down for money to build a conference center when it appeared that he'd be collecting hundreds of millions of dollars for himself. At least that way some of it would do some good.

But she couldn't rob his employees of money they'd earned. Holding him to that promise would have put her on the same level as Ned Marsh—wanting to benefit from something she hadn't worked for. And even though her cause was a good one, while Ned Marsh's request had been purely selfish, she didn't like the resemblance.

Besides, she thought, she and Zeke had made that deal when they both thought it might take three months of pretense to convince Tiffany. It was quite likely that Zeke thought the few days Dana had actually invested hadn't earned that sort of payout—and she couldn't exactly argue with that conclusion.

"He never promised, exactly," she said carefully.

Barclay gave a disgusted-sounding sigh.

"How are things going with the Rowe Foundation?"

He shifted his weight from one foot to the other, and he didn't look directly at her.

"Well, Tiffany's very busy these days, of course."

No doubt she is, Dana thought, *with Zeke's business to coordinate into her existing one.* "Well, I'm sure these things take time to arrange. I must stop monopolizing you, Barclay—you have so many guests to attend to."

With a breath of relief, she crossed the room to where Professor Wells stood beside the mantel. At last month's party, the fires had been more for looks than for serious warmth, but tonight the intense dry heat would be welcome to help drive out the chilly damp of the outside air.

Professor Wells saluted Dana with her glass. "Glad you came over. I need to talk to you about the Academic Honors Bowl."

Dana frowned. "I thought we'd finished all that up a couple of weeks ago."

"We did. It's next year's I'm talking about."

"Really? I thought you said you were retiring."

"Oh, you know how it is—these things are like childbirth. As soon as it's over you forget all the horrible pain and exhaustion and start thinking about doing it again. Sorry, I shouldn't tell you that and scare you to death just now.''

It took effort for Dana to keep her voice casual. ''By now, everybody on campus must have heard the rumor that I'm pregnant.''

Professor Wells' eyebrows rose. ''It's only a rumor?''

''I'm afraid so.'' It was a conventional reply—just a casual expression. But hearing herself say the words made Dana ache even worse, because she had to admit that part of her wished the story was true. At least then she'd have a part of Zeke to keep forever....

Foolish, of course. She didn't believe in deliberately bringing up a child without a father. Besides, she told herself with an effort at lightness, she was having enough trouble keeping Rhino in food, and if she could hardly afford Zeke's dog, she certainly didn't have the resources to raise his child.

No matter how much she'd like to have the opportunity.

Dana said firmly, ''You were talking about the academic bowl before I changed the subject.''

Professor Wells nodded at someone across the room. "I have to admit that if we're going to have the big new conference center, it might actually be fun."

"I wouldn't bet my life on getting it," Dana said glumly. Unless Tiffany and the Rowe Foundation came through for Barclay…

That response of Barclay's had been very strange, she thought. If there had been any hint of hopeful news, Barclay would have been blaring it from the rooftops. Of course, it did take more time for a foundation to act than for an individual to make a decision about a gift. And Tiffany was without a doubt busier than ever before. But still, what would it take for her to set things in motion? Not much more than a phone call—and surely she could find time for that.

"Well, I wasn't counting on it exactly," Professor Wells said. "The other reason I'm signing on is that I'd feel guilty if I abandoned you and you were stuck in Dressler Hall again."

Dana shrugged. "We did it once. We could do it—"

Uneasiness swept over her, and the hair on the back of her neck stood on end. That was very peculiar; she hadn't felt that way since—

She looked over her shoulder and felt as if time had collapsed. Zeke was standing in the arched doorway between drawing room and hall. But this time his hair wasn't touched with gold light as if he were wearing a halo.

Deliberately, Dana turned back to Professor Wells. She wasn't the hostess this time. She didn't have to greet Zeke; she didn't even have to acknowledge his presence.

Only…why was he here?

She took a firm hold on her composure. "Unless you're planning on an even larger group next year," she said.

But Professor Wells didn't seem to hear. She was looking beyond Dana, so it really wasn't a surprise a moment later when Zeke said, "Hello, Professor. Dana—may I have a moment?"

She closed her eyes for an instant and then turned to him with a smile. "I didn't know you were on the invitation list tonight."

"Or you'd have stayed home?" he asked. "That's why I crashed the party."

"I'm sure Barclay won't mind."

"No, I don't think he will at that. I have something for you." He reached into the inside breast pocket of his blazer and pulled out an envelope.

A divorce decree, Dana thought. *The thing I told him I wanted most.*

But that wasn't possible—there hadn't been time, and she hadn't received any notice of such an action. He couldn't divorce her without letting her know.

She slid a fingertip under the flap of the envelope and pulled out a slip of heavy paper. It was a cashier's check, made out to Dana Mulholland, for the sum of ten million dollars.

She wanted to cry. She wanted to curse. She wanted to crumple the check up in a ball and ram it down his throat.

Her voice shook. "I told you that you didn't have to do this."

"I remember. The money's yours, Dana. Do what you like with it."

She raised her chin. Her eyelids stung with tears. "Don't you dare patronize me by saying I earned it, Zeke."

"I wouldn't insult you that way." He raised a hand to her face, brushing the side of his index finger along the line of her jaw. Then he turned away and an instant later he was gone, leaving silence in his wake.

Barclay hurried over. ''I turn my back for a minute… What happened, Dana? Why did he leave so suddenly?''

No one else, not even Professor Wells, had seen what was written on the slip of paper. Dana reached for a handkerchief and, as discreetly as she could, tucked the check away deep into her trouser pocket.

The money's yours. Do what you like with it.

Zeke expected that she would build the conference center, of course. He probably figured that the moment he was out of sight she would wave the check under Barclay's nose and celebrate her triumph.

But in fact, right now she wouldn't be able to bear the clamor and the hubbub, the questions and the explanations, that would arise if she handed that check to Barclay. As a matter of fact, she had to admire Zeke, in a way—he'd found a very tidy method to keep himself out of the spotlight. Give the money to Dana, and let her deal with all the attention instead.

But not tonight. She simply couldn't stand it all tonight. Tomorrow would be soon enough to announce that the university would get its conference center after all.

By tomorrow, perhaps she could be happy about the gift, and perhaps she could forget the circumstances surrounding it. Forget that he had been so unwilling to have a private conversation with her that he had braved Barclay, the university's board of directors, and the crowd at Baron's Hill in order to hand her that check.

Though she had been one of the last to arrive, Dana was among the first group to leave the cocktail party. She turned down Professor Wells' offer of a ride home, saying that she felt like walking. Perhaps if she walked far enough, she might sleep more easily tonight.

The breeze turned the damp air into a weapon, slicing at her skin. Dana ducked her face into the long scarf she'd wrapped around her neck, dug her hands into her coat pockets, and started toward home, listening to the soothing rhythm of her footsteps clicking against the pavement. She had almost passed a car idling at the stop sign when she realized it was a silver Jaguar.

The engine died and the driver's door opened. For an instant Dana thought of running, but then common sense reasserted itself. She couldn't possibly outrun Zeke. Even worse, what if she ran and he didn't bother to try to catch her? She could think of nothing more humiliating.

She faced him. ''Changed your mind about the check, Zeke?''

''I assume it's too late for that.''

She didn't correct him. ''Then what is it you want?''

''To talk to you.''

''Funny. I didn't get that impression at all back at Baron's Hill. You seemed anxious to escape.''

''You were obviously just about to explode. I thought it would be safer for everybody if I got out of there before I set off the shrapnel.''

Dana shrugged. ''Why would I explode? Ten million dollars is hardly something to be angry about. You're sure you didn't run because you were afraid I might do something stupid like hug you instead?''

''I wanted to give it to you publicly so you'd get all the credit—so Barclay couldn't steal your thunder.''

"I see." She felt very tired, all of a sudden. "Our deal wasn't for ten million dollars, Zeke. Tiffany must have been very agreeable about the final terms."

"No. In fact, she wasn't agreeable at all."

"But the money..." She stuck her hand deep into her trouser pocket, needing to confirm for herself that the check was still there, that it was real. The edge of the envelope was stiff and almost sharp against her fingertips. "You don't mean you gave in? I know you said it was worth some personal sacrifice to sell your company to Tiffany, but I can't believe you agreed to work for her after all that." She tried to laugh. "I thought sleeping with me was enough of a sacrifice for you to make."

She was shivering, more from nerves than the breeze, and she couldn't stop herself.

Zeke opened the car door. "You're cold. I'll drive you home."

It was clearly an order, and Dana got in.

He started the engine. "You believe that I thought sleeping with you was a sacrifice?"

She didn't look at him. "One night with me and you were so anxious to cut a deal that you agreed to Tiffany's terms. Sounds to me like it shook you up pretty badly.''

''I didn't agree to Tiffany's terms.''

''Then what... Where did the money come from?''

He didn't seem to hear the question. ''But you're right that sleeping with you did shake me up pretty badly.''

What exactly did that mean? Not that he wanted to repeat the mistake, that was sure.

Dana sat silent until the Jaguar pulled into her driveway. ''Thank you for bringing me home, Zeke.''

She was halfway to the porch when she realized he'd shut the car off and followed her. She turned on the bottom step. ''Look, there's no point to this. There's nothing to say.''

''You asked where the money came from. I assumed that meant you want to know. Or doesn't ten million bucks even get me a cup of coffee as a token of thanks?''

She tried to smother a sigh as she pulled out her keys and climbed the steps. An unusual shadow beside the door caught her eye and she gasped.

On one end of the porch, facing toward the street, hung a porch swing. In the dim light the wood looked like teak, and the cushions were striped in jade green and pumpkin. Exactly like the swing she had once told him she wanted.

She wheeled around to look at Zeke.

"The ten million is for the conference center," he said quietly. "The porch swing is for you."

She was trembling so violently that she could hardly get the key into the lock.

"I watched you leave tonight. Lou told me where you'd gone, so I put up the swing and then came to find you." He took the keys out of her hand.

From inside the house came a single deep warning bark as Rhino defended his territory.

"The dog's still here?" Zeke sounded astonished.

"Nobody ever called to claim him."

He pushed the door open and for a couple of minutes was fully occupied by Rhino, who was displaying his joy and threatening every lamp and ornament in the living room in the process.

Dana went on to the kitchen. She had just turned on the coffeepot when Zeke came in, the dog trailing happily at his heels.

"I didn't sell the company to Tiffany," he said.

Dana turned that piece of information over in her mind, and decided that she was pleased Tiffany hadn't gotten what she wanted after all—either Zeke or the business. But it really didn't make much difference. The bottom line was still the same; after spending a single night with Dana, he'd been desperate to get away from her. Still, he seemed to expect her to ask what had happened. "Why not?"

"Because that last little middle-of-the-night stunt made it pretty clear to me that nothing short of being hit by a train was going to stop Tiffany. And a couple of things you'd said—about money not being everything, and also that Tiffany would make a very bad boss—took on a whole new meaning when I looked at her in that light."

"So what did you do?"

"I considered the other offers that I'd gotten, and I made some phone calls. That's why I had to go back to Minneapolis that day—to talk to a prospective buyer, and to meet with my employees. It was their decision, too."

"You put together another deal?" She got a couple of mugs down from the cupboard. "Must have been a downright decent one."

"Not bad. My employees got less cash but better stock options. And I got ten million dollars."

Dana's hand jerked as she poured, and hot coffee sloshed across the counter and onto the floor. Rhino sniffed hopefully at the pool. "No," Dana told him. "The last thing you need, you overgrown puppy, is caffeine." She set the pot down carefully. "You got ten million on top of what you gave me tonight, you mean."

Zeke shook his head.

Dana's ears were ringing as if she'd just come out of a very loud concert. "You gave me every last cent you got from the deal? Why, Zeke?"

"I can do it all over again. I've got a bunch of good ideas."

"That's no answer."

He didn't look at her. With the edge of his thumbnail he drew a design in the spilled coffee on the counter. "That first night you made a wise-guy remark about how seeing you with

Barclay kicked my Don Quixote instincts into overdrive.''

Dana was aghast. ''You know perfectly well I would never have married Barclay!''

''Yes—and I think I knew it right away, too. You can deny it all you want to, Dana, but you're still a romantic—too much of one to settle for Barclay. The point is, even when I knew you didn't need to be rescued from him, I still wanted to protect you. It just didn't dawn on me for a while why. Not until Tiffany put her uppity little nose into our bedroom that night.''

Dana's throat felt so tight that she knew she couldn't swallow. She pushed her coffee mug away.

''When she came barging in... Her timing could have been worse, I suppose, but not by much. I couldn't expose you to that anymore.''

It was very chivalrous of him, Dana thought, to put it in those terms, instead of saying that he hadn't been quite desperate enough to keep up the act. ''I see.''

''No, I don't think you do. Until then, I'd thought it might be nice if Tiffany took her time—as long as I could spend it in bed with you. But when she did that, I realized it wasn't a game anymore. That's why I put together another deal—so you could be free.''

As if I wanted to be.

''You did it deliberately, didn't you, Dana?''

She was confused. ''Did what?''

''Made love with me. You wanted Tiffany to see—so it would be over.''

She closed her eyes and told the truth. ''I wanted it never to be over.'' *Please,* she thought. *Let it matter to him.*

Zeke didn't move, and Dana felt her heart twist as if it were a dishrag he was wringing.

''Where did we go so wrong?'' he said finally.

''Does it even matter anymore?'' She tried to blink back tears. ''We were too young. Too innocent. Too stubborn. Too stressed. Too idealistic. Take your pick.''

''I told you once that I hadn't spent the last six years regretting our breakup and plotting how to get you back. Well, I was wrong. I didn't plot, but I regretted every day without you. I didn't realize how much until I came back to you, but then it didn't take long for me to figure out how much I'd thrown away.''

Dana could hardly breathe. *But what about now?* she wanted to ask.

"Being around you—remembering why I'd fallen in love with you in the first place. But there were other things, too. The dog, as silly as it sounds. I've never had time for anything like that. And Alison, too. She made me feel old, but she also made me wonder what it would be like to have a kid. To be a soccer coach." His voice was low. "And to be the kind of husband that I wasn't able to be six years ago. Dana, if you'll let me try...let me have another chance..."

She couldn't trust what she was hearing, because she wanted him so badly. Not until she saw the pain in his eyes, and the uncertainty, was she sure that she'd heard him asking...almost pleading...

"Yes," she whispered. "Yes—if in return you'll let me try, and give me another chance."

Zeke pulled her into his arms, and she nestled down against his warmth and felt the constant ache she'd felt for the last three weeks begin to drain from her body.

His kiss was so gentle it was almost frightening. But there was a lifetime ahead to explore all the ways they could love each other.

"I have a confession, too," she said. "I think I chose Barclay to be attracted to because—"

"You were honestly attracted to him? Oh, Dana, sweetheart—"

"Let me finish. I chose him because he was impossible. I thought I was ready to move on, but in fact I was living on memories. The reason I couldn't find another man wasn't that there weren't any, it was because I didn't want anyone but you."

"I love you," he whispered.

But something was nagging at her, and finally Dana had to say it. "Zeke, I'm scared. Last time we thought it was forever, too. We thought love was enough."

"So you admit that you love me?"

"Of course I do. Haven't I said it?"

"Not yet." He laid his chin against her hair. "That last fight—do you remember how it started?"

She frowned. "Not for certain. But I remember how it ended. I thought married people should spend all their time together, and you said if being married meant being tied down like that, then you obviously weren't cut out for marriage. And I said fine, then maybe we shouldn't be married at all—''

''And neither of us had enough sense to back down. You might have been young and innocent, Dana, but I was flat-out stupid. We were different people then, darling. This time you might be the one who gets tired of me hanging around.''

She shook her head. ''I don't think so.''

''Well, I guess we'll find out in the next fifty years or so,'' Zeke said cheerfully.

She looked up at him, and felt her fear ease. ''I do love you, you know. I always have— even when I was doing my best not to think about you.'' She put her head down on his shoulder. ''What would you have done if I'd given that check to Barclay tonight?''

''I'd have started working on a good idea tomorrow morning.''

''But you know, Zeke, the deal we made was that if Tiffany paid your price you'd give me the money. So you don't actually owe me a cent.''

''I meant it, sweetheart. It's yours.''

"Still, it's not fair that you end up with nothing for your hard work."

"I'm not exactly penniless, you know. I can keep a roof over your head for a while. Then when you build the conference center for the university, you'll have job security for life—they'd never dare fire you after that—and you can take care of me. So you see I'm actually just planning ahead."

She punched him playfully in the arm. "I think I'll give half of it to the university as matching funds to build the conference center. Besides, I only asked you for ten in the first place because I was willing to settle for five."

"Did I call you a mere pirate? Dammit, Dana, you rank with the best of them—you could teach Captain Kidd a few tricks."

"And the other half—well, you'll need a place to work on those good ideas. Besides, I'd hate for Barclay to feel useless."

"Even though he is," Zeke murmured.

"If he has five million to work with, he can hit up the Rowe Foundation for the rest."

"No, he can't."

"Why not?"

"Because it turns out Tiffany's not part of that Rowe family at all. She was faking it. Will you marry me?'' Zeke murmured against her lips.

"Anything you want. Wait a minute—what did you say?''

"I asked you to marry me. Just in case a Dominican divorce turns out to be legal in Wisconsin after all.''

She put both hands against his chest and pushed. "What are you talking about? Are we divorced or aren't we?''

"I don't know, exactly. Neither did our attorney friend in the federal pen. In fact, he asked me to drop him a note when I found out for sure.''

"Don't tell me he's suffering from a conscience now. What's he going to do, write little notes of apology to all the couples he might not have gotten divorced after all?''

"I didn't ask. Anyway, you surely don't expect that I'd try to prove we were divorced when it worked out so nicely for me if we weren't. I needed your help, Dana. I didn't know then that I also wanted you. But now that I know what I want, I'm not willing to take a chance. I vote we get married again.''

"Okay,'' she whispered. And that was the last word either of them said for a very long time.

MILLS & BOON® PUBLISH EIGHT LARGE PRINT TITLES A MONTH. THESE ARE THE EIGHT TITLES FOR MARCH 2003

HOT PURSUIT
Anne Mather

WIFE: BOUGHT AND PAID FOR
Jacqueline Baird

THE FORCED MARRIAGE
Sara Craven

MACKENZIE'S PROMISE
Catherine Spencer

MAYBE MARRIED
Leigh Michaels

THE TYCOON'S PROPOSITION
Rebecca Winters

THE WEDDING CHALLENGE
Jessica Hart

ASSIGNMENT: SINGLE MAN
Caroline Anderson

MILLS & BOON®

MILLS & BOON® PUBLISH EIGHT LARGE PRINT TITLES A MONTH. THESE ARE THE EIGHT TITLES FOR APRIL 2003

THE GREEK BRIDEGROOM
Helen Bianchin

THE ARABIAN LOVE-CHILD
Michelle Reid

CHRISTMAS AT HIS COMMAND
Helen Brooks

FINN'S PREGNANT BRIDE
Sharon Kendrick

OUTBACK ANGEL
Margaret Way

HIS PRETEND WIFE
Lucy Gordon

CITY GIRL IN TRAINING
Liz Fielding

BRIDEGROOM ON HER DOORSTEP
Renee Roszel

ML

4/03